"Yo
a

He looked amu ... ce etched in lines ... preciation. "Sorry, princess, you've already had those. And don't try to tell me that you don't want me, because you do. You're as aware of me as I am of you and you know how much that is."

He watched with merciless eyes as she turned her head away, refusing to admit even to herself that he was right.

Quite calmly he finished. "Whatever we had eight years ago is still there. It's time to get rid of it. Abstinence doesn't appear to be able to do the trick, so we'll try satiation."

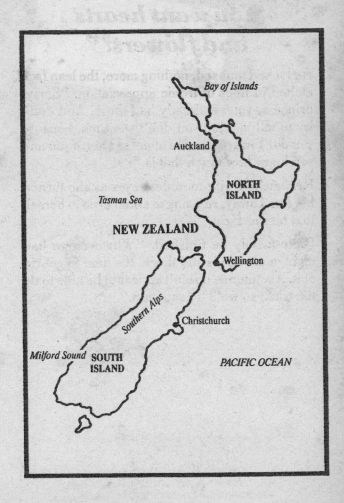

Bay of Islands

Auckland

NORTH ISLAND

Tasman Sea

NEW ZEALAND

Wellington

Southern Alps

Christchurch

Milford Sound **SOUTH ISLAND**

PACIFIC OCEAN

ROBYN DONALD

The Stone Princess

Harlequin Books

TORONTO • NEW YORK • LONDON
AMSTERDAM • PARIS • SYDNEY • HAMBURG
STOCKHOLM • ATHENS • TOKYO • MILAN
MADRID • WARSAW • BUDAPEST • AUCKLAND

Harlequin Presents first edition August 1993
ISBN 0-373-11577-6

Original hardcover edition published in 1991
by Mills & Boon Limited

THE STONE PRINCESS

CHAPTER ONE

SHE met him on her eighteenth birthday.

It had all the hallmarks of romance, that meeting. Petra Stanhope was standing on the small bridge over the lily-pond, a summer moon transforming her hair from its normal dark blonde to an ethereal silver. Floating blue chiffon deepened her changeable blue-green eyes to a brilliant sapphire. Unconsciously posed like a nymph of old, she extended a slender bare arm to rest her hand on the rustic balustrade. The graceful folds of the dress made the most of her rather too thin figure, the kindly moon glamorised her serene, regular features.

When she had dressed for her party she had been thrilled by the older, more sophisticated look created for her by her aunt's hairdresser. The classical knot on the top of her head, with a few curly tendrils falling past her cheeks to nestle confidingly on her slender neck, suited her as well as her birthday present from her aunt and uncle—a string of magnificent rose pearls.

And, in spite of her initial reservations, the blue dress was perfect. Aunt Kath was inclined to visualise her niece as only slightly older than the child she had welcomed into her home ten years ago, and choose her clothes accordingly, but this time her instincts had been right. The soft chiffon complimented Petra's angular body and arms, even lending a little substance to a bust that she had finally accepted was never going to get beyond the 'slight' stage.

Just as she had accepted that for all the neat evenness of her features, the exquisite, translucent skin she had inherited from her mother, the gentle promise of large eyes and a soft, pretty mouth, she was not considered attractive. Boys of her age preferred girls who were bright and vibrant, and Petra was essentially private, observing her world with her thoughts well hidden behind the shifting, evanescent colours of her eyes. Part of her reserve was due to her aunt's old-fashioned attitudes, part came from her early childhood when she had watched with a child's wide, innocent, but not uncomprehending gaze as her scintillating, beautiful mother danced downwards on the path that led eventually to alcoholism and a painfully pathetic death.

But tonight Petra didn't care about her inadequacies. For the first time she felt an adult.

And she had been treated as one; boys she had known for years were flatteringly surprised by this new Petra, treating her with an eager gallantry that brought wry amusement as well as a glow of pleasure to her tranquil face. Even her uncle, who had been distant and a little morose for the last few months, had cheered up. Now, as he led yet another man across the terrace to be introduced, he was almost beaming.

'Ah, there you are, my dear,' he said jovially as he reached her. 'Cooling down, are you? Here's Caine Fleming, who works for Jim Vaughan. Caine, this is our niece, Petra Stanhope. Well, we think of her as our daughter; she's lived with us for most of her life.'

Petra looked up, up, well past her uncle's five feet eight inches into the lean, smiling face of the man beside him. Caine Fleming had the compelling, predatory beauty of a hunter, a stark, Celtic bone structure which gave him a hint of untamed arrogance that not even the disciplined curves of his mouth could wholly control. Petra held out her hand with an odd feeling of inevitability, as though she was giving her life into his strong, warm grip.

'How do you do?' she said unevenly, striving to hide a paralysing shyness with her normal composure. She was relieved when he let her hand go.

'How do you do?' There was laughter in the deep, assured voice, laughter and something else that sent a tiny skip of apprehension along her nerves.

'You're cold,' Uncle Laurence said, eyeing her with concern. 'Come on in, my dear. Your aunt was wondering where you had got to.'

'It was so hot in there.' Did her voice sound as shaken as she thought it did?

'It's all that modern gyrating and wriggling they call dancing,' Uncle Laurence said, but indulgently. 'Give me a good, old-fashioned waltz any day! Come on, let's go inside.'

As she went obediently with them into the big ballroom, Petra wondered why Uncle Laurence had sought her out to present Caine Fleming.

Of course she had heard of him; her uncle had fulminated often enough about jumped-up upstarts who thought that playing the money-market gave them the right to dictate terms to anyone who was foolish enough to listen. Caine Fleming had come from nowhere to a position of considerable power and influence in Vaughan's old established merchant bank. Uncle Laurence had called him a yuppie, pronouncing the word with loathing, then gone on to dwell on those magic terms 'breeding' and 'taste', implying that Caine Fleming had neither.

But then, Uncle Laurence had complained so much lately; he had been almost paranoid ever since the last election. Nothing the new government did found favour with him; he spent long hours criticising politicians who changed all the rules as soon as they got into power, lowering tariffs to allow a flood of cheap goods into New Zealand without let or hindrance, sending old established businesses to the wall.

Alarmed by his bitterness, Petra had asked tentatively whether the well-established furniture manufacturing plant that he had inherited from his father was suffering under the new regime. He had almost bitten her head off, snapping that he knew how to deal with arriviste politicians, his father had handed the firm on to him in good repair, and he intended to do the same to his heir.

Petra had subsided because she was her uncle's heir, and she didn't want him to think that she was showing an unseemly interest in her heritage. But she was worried. She owed him and her aunt so much—her home, her happiness, the advantages they had given her...

But now, as she walked back between the two men, it was not of her uncle's strictures that she was thinking. Her wayward mind was considering how dynamic the man on her other side looked in his dinner-jacket, the austere black and white of the evening clothes suiting the lithe lines of his figure to perfection.

Compared to most girls of her age Petra knew she was remarkably unsophisticated. Her aunt and uncle were very protective, and because she loved them and was eternally grateful to them she had accepted their standards and shibboleths with resignation, if not serenity.

But now she was made restless by a sudden thunder in her blood, a wildness that called into question all her aunt's rules, and, when they reached the light of the ballroom and she looked up at Caine Fleming, she lost herself entirely in eyes as clear and sharp as ice crystals, of a grey so pale they were transparent, strange, magnetic, magician's eyes in the arrogant angles of his face.

Sudden colour scorched her cheekbones; she couldn't drag her gaze away, assailed by an odd disconnected feeling as though she had been snatched from reality and catapulted into another dimension.

The band struck up, and Caine Fleming asked in his smooth deep voice, without the broad New Zealand twang she had expected from her uncle's snobbish comments, 'May I have this dance, Petra?'

Smiling, she went into his arms as though she belonged there. At over six feet he was at least six inches taller than she; he had the wide shoulders and long legs of an athlete. Nevertheless, she fitted as though she had been made for his embrace, adjusting lightly to his hard body, her feet moving in perfect unison with his.

Petra's grace was inborn, but it had been refined by careful instruction. Caine Fleming danced with a natural ease that no amount of coaching could have produced. It was a part of the loose-limbed masculine suppleness she had noticed out in the moonlight, where she had subconsciously seen so much.

He didn't seem to want to talk, which was just as well because her mouth was oddly dry, and in spite of the singing alertness through her body she was enveloped in a strange but pleasant languor. Instinct warned her that it would be far too revealing to close her eyes, so she contented herself with staring through silky lashes at the excellent material of his dinner-jacket.

His clothes had been made for him by a very good tailor, she decided, trying to infuse some trace of objectivity into her thoughts. Petra had learned to recognise good tailoring, just as she had been taught to behave beautifully in any situation. Being ladylike, her aunt called it, and, though it was the fashion to laugh at such out-dated training, Petra had only to recall her mother, who had been not in the least ladylike, to know which she preferred.

'How old are you this birthday?' the deep voice asked, banishing the bleak memories.

Petra sighed. 'Eighteen,' she admitted. Caine Fleming was near thirty, she guessed, and those strange, colourless eyes had seen more of the world than she was ever likely to.

She risked a glance upwards. Sure enough his smiling, sensual mouth had quirked, and she thought she discerned an enigmatic irony in the cool clarity of his gaze.

'Are you still at school?'

Wistful amusement glimmered in her smile. 'No, I left at the end of last year.'

'And what are you doing now?'

A small frown pleated the straight line of her thin brown brows. 'My aunt wants me to stay home,' she said slowly. 'Just for this year.'

'But what do you want?'

She shrugged, her lashes falling to veil her emotions. 'I suppose I'll do what she wants,' she said reluctantly. 'My aunt and uncle have been very good to me.'

'Yes, you're an orphan, aren't you?'

'More or less,' she murmured. 'My mother is still alive.'

'Is she here tonight?'

'No.' Just a syllable, but it hurt. He had the perception not to pursue the matter, for which she was profoundly grateful.

Another couple, executing a flashy turn, jostled Caine from behind. He extricated them with grace, and during the laughing apology from the other man Petra saw the woman, the older, rather flamboyant sister of one of her school friends, look long and deliberately at Caine.

He met the unwavering assessment with aloof composure, something like a cynical appreciation gleaming in his glance as it rested for just a moment on the woman's soft, full mouth before flicking up to meet her eyes. Jan Pollard smiled, a sleepy, feline, almost reminiscent smile. Although they didn't exchange a word it was clear that they knew each other well. A pang of emotion so intense that she almost gasped arrowed through Petra, lodging in her heart.

'What is it?' Caine asked, looking down, the colourless eyes wiped of everything but concern.

She shook her head, sensing that the unknown emotion was jealousy, and that she couldn't let him see it.

He smiled, and she forgot about Jan, forgot that this was her birthday, forgot everything but the sheer fascination of Caine's smile, the effortless magnetism that overruled all logic and reason. Dimly she thought that if that smile had been meant for her, instead of merely humouring her, she would be like the princess in the fairy-tale, leaving all that she loved, all that she valued to follow him over the world.

'Petra,' he said softly, suddenly serious, 'I wish you were five years older.'

She knew what he was implying. Prudence, of which she perhaps had more than her share, told her that he was right. This powerful pull she felt was not going to lead anywhere. But rebellion sparked in her eyes, kindling them for a second to blue fire as startling as it was unexpected.

'Oh,' he murmured, an oblique smile pulling at his beautifully sculptured mouth. 'Not such a docile little princess, after all?'

It seemed he could read her mind, too. Flushing, unable to think of a sophisticated answer, she looked away to see her uncle smiling benignly from the side of the room.

Which was odd. She would have expected Laurence Stanhope to bristle with barely hidden antagonism instead of overt encouragement.

'I'm not in the least rebellious,' she said seriously, 'but I don't think I like being called docile. It sounds—weak and pathetic.'

Laughter lifted his chest, and Petra was seized with the desire to touch him, to discover whether the golden-brown skin of his throat was as sleek and smooth to the touch as it looked. She had to curl long thin fingers into her palms to stop the urge. Colour sizzled along her cheekbones. The odd feeling of disassociation increased, along with a *frisson* of excitement.

'Princess,' he said on an odd note, 'I don't think you're weak or pathetic; I think you're dangerous.'

Sure that he was mocking her, Petra glanced up sharply. But, although his cheeks were creased into two pronounced lines, and the wide, hard mouth was tilted into a mocking smile, there was no amusement in his expression. Instead it was disciplined into a hardness belied only by glittering points of light in his gaze.

That was when she realised that the attraction wasn't just on her side, but that he felt it, too. And that he was going to fight it because she was too young.

'An eighteen-year-old can't be dangerous,' she muttered, scarcely aware of what she said.

'Eve was dangerous immediately she'd been created,' he pointed out.

She flinched. 'That's hardly a compliment.'

'Princess,' he drawled, 'if it's compliments you want you had better ask someone else. And don't look at me with those great wounded blue eyes; they make me forget what I'm supposed to be doing. You wouldn't like it if I tripped and flung you on to the floor.'

She laughed, because he moved with a hunter's supple authority, and in a voice that didn't sound like hers she objected, 'I don't think anything could make you lose your footing. You move too easily.'

One brow shot up. 'Don't you believe it,' he said with a twisted smile. 'If he doesn't watch his step any man is capable of coming a cropper.'

The music died away, and she allowed him to escort her off the floor, knowing that he was going to leave her and never come back because he thought she was too young.

Quickly, without giving herself time to realise what she was doing, Petra asked, 'Will you be at the Hudsons' party tomorrow night?'

'No,' he said, his withdrawal as sudden and as shocking as a bucketful of icy water in the face.

She had been forward, chasing him, and her aunt had told her that men hated that. Clearly, her aunt had been right. Producing a bright, gallant little smile Petra could only murmur inanely, 'Never mind.'

'Thank you for the dance, princess.' He gave her a long, unsettling look before relinquishing her to the custody of her aunt and uncle. For several moments he stayed chatting, apparently unaware of both her aunt's carefully hidden astonishment and the covert interest of almost every woman in the room, until he excused himself to talk to another couple not very far away.

Desperately trying to hide her humiliation, Petra smiled with the carefree gaiety her guests expected, a smile she kept pasted to her mouth as the rest of the evening dragged by. She smiled at the assortment of men she danced with, while all the time her skin checked Caine's whereabouts. With black bitterness she envied the women he danced with, and noted with angry understanding when he left with Jan Pollard. She hated the smug, anticipatory curve to the woman's lush mouth. But she kept smiling.

At last it was over. After a proud kiss Aunt Kath sent her up to bed with a command to sleep in as late as she wanted to in the morning.

Tired as Petra was, sleep was slow in coming. Lying in the pretty room her aunt had redecorated for her the year before, she clamped her eyes shut and recalled every moment of the dance she had had with Caine Fleming, every expression on that hard, striking face, the hidden flames summoned by the chandeliers from the thick waves of his dark hair, his potent charisma, the cold glints in those startling eyes and the way they had warmed as they rested on her upturned face.

Fierce, unbidden excitement ate into her normal composure as she drifted off into fantasy, imagining things that made her blush, brought a reckless heat to every cell in her body...

Eventually she slept, waking to a summer's day with the sun beating down on Auckland's beautiful seascapes, so inextricably melded with the land that you had to know the place intimately to be sure which was island and which peninsula, which patch of glittering blue was sea and which was a lagoon or a lake, the drowned remnants of an explosive crater dead long ago.

With a little skip of her heart Petra realised that it was Saturday, and she didn't have to get up and go to school.

And then, with an odd pang, that she would never have to get up and go to school again. Suddenly her life seemed to stretch out before her, bleak and grey and boring.

Perhaps she should have insisted on going to university. But it had seemed little enough recompense for Kath Stanhope's devotion, this year spent 'coming out', accompanying her aunt on the many social activities with which she filled her days. She had often said how much she was looking forward to taking Petra around, speaking glowingly of the holidays they would take, the trips to Australia and further afield, the long leisurely jaunt around Europe in the northern summer...

And Petra had been looking forward to it too. Until last night, when a man's pale gaze had made her heart thump unbearably, setting off explosions in the innermost reaches of her mind.

Now, as she showered and made her bed and pulled on a pair of shorts and a T-shirt, she told herself sturdily that she would look forward to it again. An introduction in the moonlight and one dance in the arms of the most exciting man she had ever met could not be allowed to spoil her year, especially as Caine Fleming had made it clear that he was not going to pursue that wildfire attraction.

Sinking back on to the bed, she recalled with obsessive absorption the strong blade of his nose, the wide high forehead, the jutting arrogant chin, that disturbing, sensuous, compelling mouth, yet of more impact than all of those the blazing intelligence in the unusual eyes...

'Petra?'

Guiltily she jumped to her feet, calling, 'I'm coming, I'm coming.'

Her aunt opened the door, her smile fading a little when she caught sight of her niece. 'Darling, I hope you aren't going to wear those shorts to breakfast. You know your uncle doesn't like bare knees at the table. How would you like to go out on the Donaldsons' yacht? Mary has just rung and said that as it's such a lovely day they've decided to take a run up to Kawau.'

'I'd love to,' Petra said, trying to sound enthusiastic. 'Are you coming?'

'Yes, darling, and your uncle says he'll come too!'

This was an unexpected pleasure. For the last month or so Uncle Laurence had spent most of his time at the office, intimating before the party that he would need to go again that weekend. Petra smiled sunnily, already looking forward to the rest of the day. The Donaldsons' yacht was a huge gorgeous thing, sleek and graceful. The only drawback was that there might be no others of her age, but Petra enjoyed the company of older people, especially Sir Lionel and his wife, who were amusing and charming. And there was always the possibility that their son Johnny, an old friend of hers, would be with them.

So she said cheerfully, 'It sounds lovely. Aunt Kath, thank you so much for last night. It was—wonderful.'

Her aunt's eyes grew misty, her smile tender. 'You looked so lovely—I was so proud of you, sweetheart. When I think . . .'

She didn't need to go on. Only too well Petra remembered what a little horror she had been when she'd arrived, deposited at the age of eight on her aunt's doorstep by a mother whose addiction to romance had expanded to include alcohol and the softer drugs. Prone to tantrums, sullen and resentful, completely undisciplined, Petra had been the sort of child only a parent could love. But her separated parents were busy with their own lives, her father overseas as far as he could be from the wife who had cuckolded him into a laughing-stock, her mother too torn by demons she could not control to have time for the child she had borne.

Kath and Laurence Stanhope had opened their hearts to Petra, disciplined her kindly but firmly out of her tantrums, coaxed her down the path of courtesy and politeness, and through all the turbulence of a vicious custody case, loved her. Starved for affection, she had responded like a late-blooming flower, trying her utmost to live up to their expectations.

'I was an awful child,' Petra said now, kissing her aunt's cheek, 'and when I think of what could have happened to me my blood runs cold. My fairy-godmother was working overtime when she found you for me.'

Aunt Kath laughed. 'Darling, I'll admit that you were a horror, but it didn't take us long to see that underneath the little savage there was something of your father, some good Stanhope blood! All it needed was discipline and—well, I won't say it was easy, you led us an awful dance, but it was definitely worthwhile. Come and have some breakfast, Pet, as soon as you've changed. We're to meet the Donaldsons down at the marina in an hour.'

Also meeting the Donaldsons was Caine Fleming, as magnetic in shorts and a polo-shirt that revealed sleekly muscled thighs and shoulders as he had been the night before in his austerely tailored dinner-jacket.

Petra's first artless joy was immediately dissipated as she flinched at the impact of his eyes and read surprise, and a hint of knowing derision. Her stomach plummeted nauseatingly. He thought she had engineered this meeting!

Stiffening her spine, she called on all her poise to give him a coolly distant smile before she stepped lightly from the jetty on to the deck of the yacht, laughing up into Johnny Donaldson's face as he made a production of catching her.

Just in case Caine needed the point reinforced she sat as far away from him as possible, and the minute the yacht had pulled away from the marina asked Sir Lionel if she could help put the sails up. Her aunt made a little face, but, in spite of the older woman's conviction that such behaviour was tomboyish, Petra held firm. She enjoyed sailing, loved the way the magnificent yacht quivered as the engine was cut, and the sudden, heart-lifting silence, the swift hardening of purpose as the craft united with the elements it had been created for. And this time it would take her out of reach of Caine's cool, cutting survey.

'OK,' Sir Lionel said indulgently. 'Go up and help Johnny.'

The sun gilded her bent head as they worked with the thin synthetic material, saying little while they clipped it on to the pulley and hauled it up. When it was done Johnny remarked casually, 'I'm going up to the Bay of Islands next weekend for their regatta. Why don't you come?'

Petra would have loved to have gone, but she knew that her aunt would never permit it. And she could not hurt her by insisting on her right to that sort of freedom. 'Next year, perhaps,' she said, biting back a sigh.

Johnny knew her circumstances well. He shrugged. 'Reckon she might have let you out of the cocoon by then?'

'She's over-protective, but she doesn't know how to be anything else. She grew up when girls were cherished and guarded, and she thinks that's the way it is still.'

'Not all of them. I know my mother got about a bit,' Johnny argued. He looked behind her. 'Oh, hi, Caine.' A trace of hero-worship coloured his voice. 'How's the money-market?'

'Volatile,' Caine said drily, coming to a halt just behind Petra.

She didn't turn around, but the hairs on the back of her neck stood up in a primitive warning.

Suddenly speculative, Johnny eyed Petra's carefully blank face. 'As usual. But you know how to manage it, don't you? My father says you're the eighth wonder of the world. Says it needs nerve and guts and intuition to play the markets like you do. As well as a sort of divine arrogance.' He pulled a wry face. 'Looks like I'll just have to settle down to being a doctor.'

'A doctor,' Petra said sweetly, 'helps people.'

Johnny laughed and gave an affectionate tug to a satiny lock of hair above her ear. 'Oh, certainly, but being a doctor's hardly romantic, is it?'

'And you think playing the market is?' Caine's voice was dry. 'Don't believe it. It's hard work, just like any other. And it's a young man's game. I'm thinking of packing it in.'

Johnny's eyes opened in surprise, but after a moment spent surveying Caine's face he grinned. 'Nah,' he drawled, 'you won't give it up. My father says it's an addiction, it gets in your blood. He thinks you'll go a long way, right to the very top.'

'The top of what?' Caine asked. He was smiling, Petra could tell, but there was something very remote in the deep, confident voice, something as self-sufficient as an eagle winging alone through the empty skies of a world that valued the kill more than the hunt.

Caine didn't, she thought with an unnerving flash of insight. To him the hunt was all, the material rewards pleasant but not the reason he risked bankruptcy and burn-out.

'Whatever you want.' Johnny grinned, easy and uncomplicated. 'The sky's the limit,' he said, and laughed. 'It always is to you entrepreneurs, isn't it? Ah, well, I guess there's no place for us, the ones that never aspire to much more than keeping our heads above water, eh, Pet?'

'Pet?'

She braced herself at the subtle note of mockery in the cool, uninvolved tone. 'It's short for Petra,' she said stiffly as Johnny directed a teasing grin her way and leapt athletically down to the cockpit. 'I don't like it.'

It was something she had just discovered, and the surprise of her discovery was in her voice, rendering it, she thought with despair, childishly petulant.

'I can't say that I blame you. Although you are a little like a pet—sweet and friendly, loved and stroked, and not expected to do anything other than return uncritical adoration.'

'That,' she replied, hurt and bewildered by the bite in the words, 'is unkind. Who told you that?'

His attack had brought her quickly around to face him. Wounded, she caught an odd expression on his face—amused yet cynical. 'Oh, it was Jan, I suppose,' she said, trying to hide the ugly pain of jealousy with worldliness. Counterfeiting a smile, she added. 'She doesn't like me much. She thinks I'm prissy and stuck-up.'

He was watching her through narrowed eyes, the depthless transparence of his gaze oddly intimidating. 'Hmm, perhaps Princess does suit you better than Pet.'

It stung, as she suspected it was meant to, but she favoured him with a serene smile which she hoped would disguise the hurt. 'Thank you.'

Her glance slid past him to her aunt, who was watching them, her brows knitted into a frown above her sunglasses. Obeying the unspoken summons, Petra ducked beneath the boom and went down to join her, breathing jerkily as though she had been teetering on the edge of some unknown abyss and had only just managed to pull herself back.

It was a ridiculous sensation, and one she squashed firmly. Determined to show Caine that she had no intention of pursuing him, she was polite for the rest of the morning, smiling at him with warmth but no invitation, making herself meet the mocking amusement in his eyes with calm dignity, acting for all she was worth so that he wouldn't realise how his presence churned her emotions into turmoil.

By lunchtime they were anchored a hundred metres off one of the small beaches that dimpled the sheltered inner coast of Kawau Island. The pale half-moon of sand was guarded by the gaunt, tall finger of a ruined tower, one of the buildings at the old copper mine. South Harbour ran gently into the interior of the island, and on the horizon, not too far away, the mainland stretched out hazed in greens, the hills rising behind to a mysterious indigo.

It was the perfect picnic: delicious food, amusing and intelligent company, and the day like a blue and gold symphony bestowed by a generous summer. Cicadas trilled in the trees, and tiny waves lapped gently against the beach, while behind them a steep, pine-clad hill rose to cut off any vagrant southerly breezes. Petra ate sparingly and listened, contributing whenever it was needed, trying to convince herself she was enjoying herself.

She kept her eyes carefully away from the lean figure of Caine, who lounged with pagan grace against the trunk of the tree, somehow making every other man appear at once ordinary and clumsy. He was like a sleek golden panther in a group of cattle, she thought fancifully, sneaking a sly peep from beneath the silky screen of her lashes; he was well-fed at the moment, but with the aura of danger stark about his lean, well-muscled body.

The angular, intelligent face suddenly hardened as he caught her eye. Colour heated her cheeks, and her glance slid sideways to catch her uncle watching her with tightened lips. Yet he smiled, as though he was pleased with her.

A tiny frown pulled Petra's thin brows together. Deep inside her a small chunk of ice coalesced. She looked around the group of people she had known for years, and it was as if they were strangers, indifferent, pedestrian. Tension crawled across her skin like a loathsome insect. With determination she banished the stupid foreboding and, turning to the woman beside her, began to use the social skills her aunt had so painstakingly taught her, ignoring Caine's enigmatic scrutiny in the common coinage of light, amusing conversation.

After lunch they swam.

'I'm going to sunbathe,' one of the younger women, running an idle hand down her sleek, lush curves, announced when they were back on shore. 'Coming, Petra?'

Petra finished drying herself off, and screwed her hair up into a pony-tail. All the time they had been in the water she had carefully not looked at Caine, had stayed out of his way, yet she had known exactly where he was and knew, too, that he was watching her.

She wished that she had a figure that looked good in swimsuits. Unfortunately the prevailing fashion for sleek bikinis emphasised every angle of shoulder and hipbone, every deficiency in breast and buttocks. Petra was not going to lie in the sun where everyone could see that compared to Fiona Hayward—or Jan Pollard—she had an androgynous body, more like a boy's than a woman's.

'No, I want to see if I can sneak up on a wallaby,' she said with what she hoped was a casual, off-hand air. 'Coming, Johnny?'

'Too hot,' he said firmly.

'Too lazy,' she teased.

He grinned and rolled over on to his stomach. 'Yep.'

After tossing another comment on his lack of energy, and promising her aunt that she wouldn't get lost and would take care not to fall over a cliff, she ran lightly across the hot sand and into the deep, drowning shade of the pine trees.

Beneath them, where the zithering of the cicadas reached a dizzying crescendo, it was pleasantly cooler. Petra walked stealthily along the faint tracks worn in the slippery needles by the wallabies—small kangaroo-like animals that had been released on the island from Australia over a hundred years ago. The clean scent of the pines mingled with the salt essence of the sea, astringent, stimulating.

She needed the time away from Caine Fleming; whenever she closed her eyes she could see him, the sensuous pull and play of muscles beneath teak-brown skin, wide shoulders and lean hips above strong thighs, and the elegant spareness and symmetry, all male in its primitive appeal. As well as the sheer power and strength that clung to him like an aura.

He contrasted too much with the other men, most of whom were a little flabby from their indoor jobs. Even Johnny, young and fit as he was, didn't have that air of arrogant masculine competence.

Petra found a small flat patch of hillside, and sat down beneath a tall ponga, the airy fronds of the tree-fern drooping in the still air above her little bower. Through the branches of the pines she could see the blue-green glimmer of the bay, and if she listened very carefully she could hear laughter through the stridulations of the cicadas, the distance and her own unsettled emotions transforming it into something mysterious, other-worldly.

A dryad in ancient Greece might have felt like this when she heard Ulysses—half-hero, half-pirate, all man—land on a beach in the Golden Ages, she thought fancifully, resting her forehead on the arms looped about her knees. Cicadas sizzled about her, still, warm air freshly scented with balsam caressed her skin.

Sleep beckoned, but the hairs along her arms and at the back of her neck began to rise, pulled taut by some inchoate foreboding. In answer to their summons she lifted her head to see Caine come up the hill, long legs striding purposefully, his head carried high.

And she knew immediately that this was what she had wanted ever since she had seen him in the moonlight— to be alone with him.

'Your aunt thought you might get lost,' he said lightly, coming to a stop in front of her.

Petra looked up into eyes as clear as spring-water, unreadable, oblique. A delicious sense of helplessness weakened her limbs, a kind of thrill rooted in the most primitive part of her personality.

'I'm not in the habit of getting lost,' she replied huskily, giving him the chance of staying—or going.

His mouth curved in an ironic little smile as he sat down beside her, close, yet not touching. 'There might always be a first time,' he murmured gravely.

Words dried in her mouth. She didn't know whether she should forget last night's painful rebuff, or whether his unexpected appearance meant that he had decided to make amends.

She said, 'Did you sleep with Jan?' And could have died with horrified embarrassment.

He responded calmly, 'No, although I intended you to believe that I was going to.'

Petra bit her lip. 'I didn't,' she insisted in a muffled voice, astounded because until that moment she thought she was convinced he had spent the night with Jan. 'But I was jealous anyway.'

There was a pause, heavy with unspoken thoughts, breathless with taut expectancy. He said roughly, 'I'm too old for you.'

'I'm too young for you,' she corrected, knowing it was true.

'Petra, look at me. The line of your cheek is enchanting, but I want to see your eyes.'

Blushing, she lifted her face for his inspection, her gaze meeting his steadily. His eyes had darkened, the pupil swallowing up the transparent iris, and she saw a flush of colour along his autocratic cheekbones.

'What am I going to do with you?' he asked unevenly.

She summoned up all her nerve, looking at him with desperate courage, her own skin heating at the naked demand she read in his expression. 'I don't know,' she said hesitantly. 'I—don't want to be a nuisance, but I don't know what to do about this. I don't even know what it is.'

'Oh, princess,' he said with a wry, crooked smile, closing his eyes for a second. When he opened them again they were hard and blazing with a clear fire. He bent his head and kissed her soft, untutored mouth.

It was like an explosion of fireworks, only they were in her blood and behind her closed eyes, in the soft skin of her lips, gathering in a riot of sensation at her breasts and the juncture of her thighs. His mouth was warm and gentle and insistent; Petra could feel the contact from her head to the tips of her toes. Sparks of emotions shot through her. She gave a funny little choked moan, and the gentle pressure increased.

Her heart thundered in her breast, mingling with the muted tattoo of his. He lifted his head to stare down into her blindly seeking face, said something she had never actually heard pronounced before, then, as if driven by forces beyond the strength of his will, his mouth crushed down on to hers again, forcing it open in a kiss that bore about the same resemblance to the previous one as a blizzard did to a snowflake.

Somehow her hands clenched into fists on his shirt, pulling him closer. Petra had been kissed before, she had even suffered a French kiss from one of her friends' brothers, but she had hated it and made sure she was never inveigled into that sort of experimentation again.

But this, this was different!

Her body melted, flamed in the heat that rippled through nerves and cells, arrows of fire homed in with merciless accuracy, pooling at the fork of her body, enticing her breasts into a sensual conspiracy so that when his arms crushed her against his lean, hard torso she gasped again in an anguish of pleasure.

Still with his mouth on hers he rolled backwards, pulling her on top of him, his lean, strong hands holding her imprisoned. But oh, such a willing captive! She should have been shocked, but the hard heat of his body beneath hers sent chills up her spine, and without realising what she was doing she arched herself against him with a passion as unhindered as it was new.

'Petra,' he breathed, kissing the silky length of her lashes, the slight hollows beneath her cheekbones and then the sensitive spot just below her ear.

Strong teeth nipped the little lobe, and she whimpered, nuzzling into the column of his neck, her hands easing open to search beneath the soft knit of his shirt, across the hard tautness of his rib-cage to his shoulders. His skin was like oiled silk, damp and hot, netted with springy hair. Petra clung to him, stroking the taut masculine muscles with wondering delicacy, revelling in the swell and play of them as they tightened beneath her questing fingers.

His questing, demanding mouth found the sleek line of her throat, the wildly throbbing pulse at the base, then touched off explosions along the line of her collarbone.

Petra's voice came shaking through softly swollen lips when she said his name. She stared with dazed intensity down into a face drawn with passion, the autocratic features stark and tense as though he suffered the same wonderful pain that she was enduring.

As she watched he struggled to regain control, the turbulence in his eyes banished by a ferocious will that clamped down on the need and the hunger, bringing them under a fierce subjection.

'Hell!' he said explosively, his voice as shaken as hers, and he eased her out of his embrace. Sitting up, he dropped his head on to the arms clamped around his knees, and dragged in deep, ragged breaths.

CHAPTER TWO

PETRA'S eyes devoured him with a drowsy, hungry gaze; she was unable to think, unable to do anything but feel. Yet slowly the humming excitement began to simmer down, and as it did embarrassment crept in like a dark smear over the lovely day. Touching her tongue to her dry lips, she winced at their tenderness, and realised with horror that she had almost begged him to make love to her. She had been forward, wanton, and Caine must be disgusted with her.

There popped into her mind a tiny cameo of a man's expression as he had looked at her mother, the sneering contempt that had rendered his handsome face ugly while Anne Stanhope had pleaded with him to stay.

'You made all the running,' he had said, cutting the recriminations short with brutal callousness. 'Women like you get what you deserve.'

Suddenly, unable to lie there any longer while Caine despised her, Petra jumped to her feet.

'No, you don't.' Caine's voice was as cold as the ice in his eyes. The fingers that manacled her wrists brought her up short with abrupt force. Effortlessly he stood up. 'What the hell was that all about?'

She stood trembling, her head lowered, afraid to look up and see the disgust in his face.

'Petra?' She shook her head, but an inexorable finger lifted her chin. He stared into her shamefaced countenance, and then he said in a different voice entirely, 'You're terrified! Did I frighten you so much, princess? I'm sorry, sweet, I—hell, I behaved like an animal, and you're not much more than a child!'

His mouth twisted as she slowly lifted flickering lashes, her gaze caught, trapped, fascinated by the flames smouldering in the crystalline depths of his eyes. She touched her tongue to her lips again, wondered at the absorption with which he followed the tiny movement, and trembled once more as she realised it aroused him. Her heart began to thump again in her chest.

She whispered, 'I don't know what happened. Caine?'

'Oh, God,' he groaned, closing his eyes for a second as he pulled her close in what he clearly meant to be a comforting grip.

Only no sooner did they touch than the same incandescence burst forth again, and they swayed together, hip to hip, thigh to thigh, pressed in a timeless embrace sanctioned since male and female had looked at each other and wanted. Until Caine tore himself free, staring down at her with an incredulity which she more than matched.

'And you don't even know how you affect me,' he said grimly. 'Or do you behave like this with every man who kisses you?'

Her eyes filled with tears, and he muttered beneath his breath, 'Princess, don't, or I'll kiss you again and, God help us both, I think I'll end up taking you here, with the sound of your aunt's voice in my ears.'

'What are we going to do?' Petra asked, unbearably stimulated by the heated passion of their embraces and the deep husky voice in which he had just said those last arousing words.

'One of two things. We can both run like hell in opposite directions, and spend the rest of our lives wondering what might have happened, or we forget the fact that I am ten years older than you, and get to know each other; slowly, and with great discretion.'

This must be how prisoners felt as they watched the jurors file back into the courtroom. Breathlessly, completely unaware of the trembling plea of lips and eyes, Petra asked, 'What—will we do?'

A smile as reckless and passionate as a buccaneer's transformed his face. 'Let's try,' he said. 'At the very least it will be excellent for my self-control. Practice makes perfect, they say. By the time we reach wherever we're headed for we should be able to move mountains by will-power alone! But we'd better get back to the beach right now.'

Acutely conscious of the soft bloom on her mouth, the dazzled light in her eyes, Petra walked beside him down the hill, emerging into sunlight so glaring that for several seconds she couldn't see properly.

When she could, she shrank at the comprehension in most of the eyes that turned to them—amusement in some, chagrin in others, a little condemnation. And swiftly hidden alarm from her aunt. There was something not quite right in her uncle's smile, yet he said nothing to her, neither then nor later.

Aunt Kath did, however, that evening when they were safely at home. 'Dear,' she began carefully, 'I don't want you to think that I don't like Caine Fleming, because I do.' She gave a faint, reminiscent smile. 'I doubt if any woman could dislike him! But I think you should know that he hasn't got a very good reputation. He's a little too masculine for his own good, and it's the way of men, you know, to take what's offered.'

Petra heard the jagged note in the words, and wondered if Uncle Laurence had ever been offered, and taken. It seemed unfair to Caine, because he hadn't; he had pulled back when he must have known that she was so far under the influence of passion that she would have given him anything he asked for.

Of course she couldn't tell her aunt that; the very thought of it was like betrayal. So she nodded, hugging the memory to her.

Her aunt went on, still in that cautious tone, 'And, of course, he's too old for you.'

'I know,' Petra said quietly.

'I'm glad.' Relief was apparent in Kath Stanhope's voice. 'He's a very clever man, and very—sexy is what you young things say, isn't it? But I think that beneath the glossy surface there are other, less sympathetic aspects to his character. I wouldn't like to make an enemy of him.' She bestowed a fond smile on Petra. 'I knew you would be sensible, darling. Now, are you ready? Your uncle's waiting, and we don't want to miss a minute of the Hudsons' party, do we?'

The Hudsons were a middle-aged couple noted for the excellence of their entertainment. Not because they spent ages thinking up outrageous themes, although they had done that on occasion. Somehow they managed to produce a mysterious alchemy at each occasion that saw everyone enjoy themselves immensely. It was a rare talent, one that Petra's mother had possessed, that ability to lift an occasion beyond the mundane into heights of extravagant pleasure.

Unfortunately Anne Stanhope had had other talents as well. Like inevitably desiring the wrong man, and making herself conspicuous.

She was a little forlorn because Caine was not going to be there, so that the excitement that surged through Petra when he appeared five minutes after she had arrived at the gracious old house up in the Waitakere ranges was pure and unadulterated.

'Hello,' she murmured, gazing up at his lean face with eyes the warm, hopeful blue of a spring sky.

'Princess.' The warm intimacy of his smile was a caress more potent than the sensation of fur on bare skin.

The evening that followed was rapturous. He made sure that there was no physical contact, not even dancing with her when late in the night someone put music on, but he stayed by her side, subtly proprietorial, and they talked as though they were the only people in the room.

Surprisingly they had a lot in common, although he was inclined to shock her with his cynicism. Enjoying his subtle mind, Petra relished stretching her own to keep up, and although she admired his incisive intellect she was not overawed by it. By the time the party ended she hoped that he was starting to see her as a human being, not merely a woman who had an uncomfortable effect on his hormones. With any luck her circumspect behaviour had dimmed his memory of the afternoon, when she had responded to him with such wanton lust.

Altogether it was a wonderful evening, even though he let her leave with her aunt and uncle, watching them go with a twisted, sardonic smile that sat easily on his hard mouth. Her aunt and uncle were silent all the way home, but, wrapped in the aftermath of the most exciting day she had ever experienced, for once Petra was not concerned about their reactions.

Still borne on a wave of exaltation, she floated up the stairs to her bedroom. Smiling dreamily, she went into her small bathroom, and unscrewed a jar of expensive cleanser. Then, jar in hand, she stared unseeingly into the mirror.

Gradually her sight cleared; she noted the dazzled gaze, the hectic flush along her cheekbones, her soft, full mouth curved in a smile that held a sensual promise. But slowly, horrifyingly, over her features were superimposed another's—older, infinitely more beautiful yet sharing an identical eager, anticipatory ripeness, the same voluptuous bloom of a woman ready for love.

Shocked, the colour driven from her skin, Petra remembered how often she had seen her mother look just like that—stimulated, hopeful, ardent. The fiery need that had raced through her in Caine's arms, the melting hunger—was that what Anne had felt each time a new lover caught her eye?

Another recollection marched remorselessly into her brain. Her mother weeping gustily when each lover left her, the bitterness and the hunger that sent her searching for another man. Anne Stanhope had been hooked on romance, on sex.

'No!' Petra said aloud, dipping a shaking finger into the cleanser, smearing it over her face with swift, fierce movements that would have horrified the woman who had taught her how to look after her skin at a very expensive modelling school.

Of course she was not like her mother. Anne's needs had been indiscriminate, whereas Petra had only ever felt this divine madness with Caine. Her hand slowed, smoothing over her skin. Dismissing her mother's face from her mind, she summoned up Caine's, using it as a talisman, lingering over the clean-cut, stark strength of his features. She rinsed the cleanser off, and stood staring warily at her now naked face, her brows furrowed, until the rattle of her healthy young stomach reminded her that she had eaten very little dinner and nothing at the party.

She pulled on her dressing-gown and smiled dreamily. I'm in love, she thought in wonder. I'm in love, and he is falling in love with me. Her future rolled out before her, sweet with promise, golden with delight. Tiptoeing silently down the stairs, she allowed her fantasies full rein.

Just before she passed the door of her uncle's study she heard his voice, defensive yet angry.

'...the only way,' he was saying. 'Believe me, Kath.'

Petra stole quietly past.

'But Petra's only a baby!' her aunt wailed.

The sound of her own name jerked Petra to a stop. Ashamed, yet intensely curious, she strained her ears. Instinct warned her that this was not the usual post-party discussion.

'Oh, she's got enough of her mother in her to know what's what.' Uncle Laurence again, his voice tinged with disgust. 'You saw her coming down the track at Kawau. Smug as a Cheshire cat, and it was obvious what they'd been doing.'

Her aunt said harshly, 'She has nothing of Anne in her! Not a thing! Any girl would be thrilled if Caine Fleming kissed her. He's the most virile male I've seen for a long time.'

'He's a jumped-up bounder.' Uncle Laurence's voice was heated. 'An opportunist with only one aim in mind—to get to the top as fast as he can. He's not going to care who he tramples on on the way, either. No breeding, no background, the son of a man who couldn't even make it as a farmer in the years when any idiot could earn a good living off a farm.'

Petra's skin went clammy. She stood as though she had been struck by lightning, knowing what was coming next. Uncle Laurence would demand that she stop seeing Caine. Her chin lifted. Much as she loved the man who had been more of a parent than her own father ever had, this time she was not going to obey him.

Aunt Kath asked in a bewildered voice, 'If you feel like that why on earth do you want to encourage him?'

'Policy,' her uncle said gruffly. 'Leave it to me, Kath, I know what I'm doing.'

Her aunt accepted that, as she accepted anything her husband told her. Petra had sometimes wondered how the woman could be so uninterested in what her husband did. She had never heard her uncle speak of the business to his wife, or her aunt ask a question about it.

However, this time her aunt said tentatively, 'But, Laurence, what if he—what if they——?'

'He won't. She's a Stanhope, she has protectors, and I am not without influence with Jim Vaughan. Fleming may be an opportunist, but he's no fool. He'll keep his hormones under control,' Uncle Laurence concluded harshly, in the tone of voice that meant the subject was closed. His voice softened. 'Now, Kath, don't you worry. Just——'

All of her appetite having completely fled, Petra turned and scuttled silently back up the stairs, thoughts ricocheting tumultuously around her head. In spite of her eavesdropping, shame was the last thing she felt. Resentment—oh, yes! Uncle Laurence had no right to say she shared certain aspects of her character with her mother! It was simply not true! And she had *not* looked smug!

But what on earth did he want from Caine? It had to be something vital for him to overlook what he considered to be Caine's deficiencies. Should she warn Caine? No, that would be the worst sort of disloyalty.

And Caine, she thought hazily, recalling the strong angles and planes of his dark face, the way he carried himself with such concentrated authority, Caine was more than capable of looking after himself.

Teeth gnawing at her bottom lip, Petra walked across to the window, and gazed down on the moonlit garden. The small bridge across the lily-pond was a dark bar against the glimmering waters. Just over twenty-four hours ago, she thought in wonder, she had met Caine for the first time on that bridge, and now she thought she might love him until the end of her life.

She hugged her arms around her slight body, lips parting in a wide, tremulous smile. Everything was suddenly appallingly complicated, but she wouldn't have it any other way, because the complicating factor was Caine.

They were inseparable for the following three weeks—a time tinged with wonder and magic for Petra, whose breathless, expectant excitement was only slightly shadowed by the fact that Caine made sure he never touched her. They went sailing on his yacht, and to the theatre, to the cinema, to dinners for two at expensive restaurants, walked in the Waitakere hills where the huge kauri trees made her feel small and unimportant. He took her to an outdoor concert in the Domain, watching with lazy, amused possessiveness while she vibrated with excitement and delight, her glowing vitality earning her sideways looks and open admiration from the crowd around. And occasionally he drove for long, silent miles through the countryside.

'That must have bored you,' he said after the first time.

Artlessly, she shook her head. How could she be bored when she was with him?

His mouth hardened, and twisted into a smile that was subtly derisive. But it appeared that the derision was directed at himself, for he said softly, 'Don't spoil me, princess. I like to drive when I'm trying to work something out. Usually it helps, gives me an idea of how to deal with the situation.'

Although he would discuss almost anything else with her, he never spoke about his emotions, or his life, so that each tiny discovery she made about him was a treasure, a sweet symbol of his growing trust.

'Did it this time?' she asked a little anxiously.

He laughed, and the rare moment of communion was gone. 'Yes, it did. Come on, I'll take you home to change, then I'll pick you up for dinner in an hour.'

But as the weeks went by into autumn she felt hunger eat into her soul, so that the meeting of their glances, the sound of her name on his lips, or his slow drawl as he called her 'princess' had the power to set flames licking through her. He fascinated her, enthralled her, turned her into a different person, all restraint and reserve banished by the overwhelming force of her love. The need he had kindled flared deep in her soul, overshadowing all the other concerns of her life so that her whole attention was focused on him. She found herself beginning to respond sharply to his teasing, then gazing at him with bewildered eyes, hating herself.

'Frustration,' he told her one day at the zoo, turning from his survey of a panther draped over a branch to watch with hooded eyes as chagrin coloured her cheeks.

She had snapped at him for no reason, and now she was stricken with remorse. And a nagging fear; she could remember just such easy grief and anger from her mother. Dumbly she looked at him, his indolent image magnified by the tears in her eyes.

'I feel it, too,' he said, a disturbing undernote of harshness in his tone. 'The torments of the damned. I lie twisting at night, imagining all the ways there are to make love to you, and I curse because I can't have you, can't take that delectable little body and make it mine.'

Desire snapped in her stomach, pulsed irresistibly through her body. Shyly, she whispered, 'Oh, yes...' Colour peaked in her cheeks as he laughed softly.

'Welcome to the world of the erotic dream, princess.'

'I thought there was something wrong with me,' she confessed, knowing that with every word she was sounding more like some naïve schoolgirl, yet unable to hold them back.

Caine's smile was edged with irony. 'No, it's just a cosmic joke, the age-old pull of the senses. Of course, if you were older the only thing to do would be to go to bed and sate ourselves,' he continued in a calm, reasonable voice. 'But we can't do that.'

Because she was too young.

'Then what are we going to do?' But Petra knew even before she spoke, and the knowledge pulled her skin tight, made her feel sick and cold and betrayed.

'I'm no masochist,' he said tautly, 'and you're not cut out for it either, so we're going to say goodbye, and we're not going to see each other again.'

She bit her lip to hold back the outcry because it would be no good; he had made up his mind. The autocratic features were harsh with a determination that was going to shatter her heart.

'Damn you and your blasted honour,' she said miserably.

He laughed softly, and it didn't help a bit that the mockery was directed at himself. 'I'm sorry. I suppose I knew right from the start that this was inevitable, but I wanted—to play in your garden for a while.'

The panther flowed from the branch like honey over a spoon, and began to pace across the floor of the cage, its eyes fixed unwinkingly on them.

'It was unfair,' Caine said, still in that same flat voice. 'But you're so sweetly innocent, so—generous. Everything I'm not. I wanted to enjoy that freshness, just for a while. But I'm not going to, not just to give myself some temporary pleasure.'

Stricken, Petra couldn't hide her flinch. 'Is that what it would be?'

'I don't know.' He watched as the panther lifted its lip in a chilling snarl. 'I'm not noted for my constancy. And you're so young—a crush is not the best foundation to build a relationship on.'

'I love you,' she said baldly.

The panther suddenly rolled over and stretched, living velvet over steel, its claws extended to their fullest extent. Petra thought dully that they were raking her heart, scarring it for life.

'I know.' He was smiling, but there was no humour in it. 'But it will die, Petra, it always does. First love is the hardest to bear, but eventually it fades. One day, in the not too distant future, you'll look back and think of yourself and me with a kind of tender amusement.'

'Don't patronise me,' she said grittily, turning on her heel to storm off, away from him, away from the panther. Two predatory animals, one inside, one outside the cage, both dangerous, she thought, aware that she was being unfair and enjoying it perversely. Both beautiful and unpredictable, but of the two the panther was the kinder because it could only kill, whereas Caine had broken her heart.

He caught her up at the gate, and took her elbow, holding her with fingers that gripped unkindly when she tried to pull away.

'Don't be childish,' he said curtly. 'You're only reinforcing what I said. One of the first things an adult has to learn to deal with is rejection.'

'I can't imagine that anyone has ever rejected you,' she blurted out, keeping her face averted.

He gave a ghost-laugh, mirthless and savage. 'I was rejected by my parents,' he said.

Her head whipped around. It was the first time he had ever spoken of his childhood. Scanning the icy withdrawal in his expression, she asked disbelievingly, 'How?'

'I was different.' The broad shoulders lifted in a dismissive shrug. 'My father worked as a sharemilker for an elderly couple without any children, and, when I was only a kid, well before I went to school, I made my way across to the boss's house. Mrs Anderson must have seen something in me because she began to read to me, and her schoolteacher's instincts were aroused when she saw that more than anything in my life I wanted to read too. So she taught me.'

'Did your mother mind?'

'No, she had three other children under the age of five. Anything that got one of us out from under her feet was welcome.' Black brows drawn together, he looked up as a cloud passed across the sun. 'We'd better get into the car, that's——'

Even as he spoke great drops hurtled down. He caught her hand and ran with her to the car, but by the time they were safely inside they were both soaked and the rain outside had settled to a downpour.

'Damn!' Caine said, fitting the key into the engine. 'I'd better get you home before you catch a chill.'

But she was shivering within minutes, even with the heater on, and he said half to himself, 'It would be better if I took you back to my place and dried your clothes there.'

Clenching her teeth to stop them chattering, Petra nodded. He lived in a villa close to the zoo, in an area that was, he said, ripe for gentrification. And therefore a good investment. He had never taken her there, so she looked around the quaint little villa with frank curiosity as he pushed her in through the front door.

Inside the walls had been stripped back to kauri matchlining which glowed with a mellow, honey-coloured lustre. The room was warm and comforting, yet subtly aloof.

'Into the bathroom,' he said, not giving her time to admire it. 'Hand your clothes out, and I'll put them in the dryer.'

Petra obeyed, and all curiosity fled as she wondered miserably what he would do if she used the occasion to seduce him. Surely, she thought, as the warm water played over her, surely he wouldn't be able to resist her if she—well, if she walked out naked? Was that what you did when you seduced someone? She bit her lip, aware that however much she wanted him she couldn't do it. Her aunt's teachings were too firmly ingrained.

When he tapped on the door she was wrapped in a large bath-sheet, drying her hair. 'Yes?' she said uncertainly.

'Are you decent?'

'Yes.' Her voice was wooden.

'Come and get your clothes.'

She opened the door and took the bundle of clothes, hoping that she would see something, some spark of emotion in his countenance. But although he didn't avoid meeting her glance his expression was completely impassive. Her lips trembled as she sent one last appealing look, only to see it break on the granite hardness of his will.

He had already cut her out of his life. Petra wanted to weep, to fling herself down on the ground and indulge in one of the tantrums that had made her a byword in her childhood; she wanted to scream and swear and hit Caine because he was not going to give in, he had the strength to say goodbye to her and make it stick. But her aunt had trained her well. Five minutes later, when she emerged sleek and shining and dressed, little of the turmoil and pain was visible in her face beyond a bleakness that leached the shifting colour from her eyes, leaving them dull and opaque.

'I'll only be a few minutes,' he said as he left the room.

Petra had to blink hard to control the tears. I will not cry, she told herself ferociously. She sat down on the sofa and stared into the flames of the fire he had lit while she showered.

Her name penetrated through layers of sleep, of exhaustion. She muttered something and snuggled deeper into the fabric of the sofa, but the persistent voice called her again, and when she still refused to wake up an uncompromising hand grabbed her shoulder and shook. Smiling, she turned her face into it.

'No,' he said thickly. 'Wake up, princess, it's time to go.'

Her mouth caressed the hard skin of his palm. She smiled drowsily and touched it with her tongue, enjoying the salty male taste, following the deeply indented lifeline down to the mound of his thumb. Her small teeth grazed the skin.

'God,' Caine muttered, and suddenly she was enveloped by his warmth, hard arms lifting her high against the rapid beating of a runaway heart. 'Why did you touch me?' he demanded, the words so guttural that she had difficulty disentangling them.

'I wanted to,' she sighed, not understanding anything beyond the fact that this was where she belonged. Turning her face into his throat, she kissed the pulse that throbbed there, her lips parting greedily so that the tip of her tongue could test with delicate delight the salty male texture and flavour.

His arms tightened, and a groan was torn from his throat. Petra looked up into a face darkened and drawn by need, stripped of its civilised veneer by the power of sensuality. Once she would have been terrified by such stark passion, but now the same hunger prowled inside her, too, so powerful that reason and logic went down before it, casualties of the primitive instinct to mate.

Caine slid her down the length of his body, watching her face with narrowed, blazing eyes. She smiled, the blind satisfied smile of a siren, and moved against his taut strength in spontaneous, involuntary excitement. Sensations swirled through her. She slid her arms around his waist and pressed harder against him, reading his response in the leaping flame in his eyes, the darkening pupils as they dilated, the slow crawl of heat along his cheekbones.

With a murmur of pleasure and anticipation she kissed his throat again, and he said something in a harsh, impeded voice, and then she was borne down on to the huge sheepskin on the floor, her mouth taken and possessed while his long fingers slid open the buttons on her shirt and spread the lapels. Petra had worn no bra beyond the slight support of a teddy, and she watched as his eyes darkened, glorying in the sudden hissing release of his breath when he pulled the tiny snaps apart, baring her breasts to his fierce survey.

A moan caught in her throat. She copied his movements, her hands feverish, then slow and sensuous as they slid with hungry pleasure over his chest, caressing him, revelling in the different textures of male and female, satin and silk, the soft furring of hair, the slight roughness of his beard on her skin.

When his mouth sought the soft mounds of her breasts Petra cried out, sensation piercing her in the most exquisite agony, her body arching into his as he found his destination, the hard roused aureole, drew it in, and suckled strongly.

She thought she might die. On fire, consumed by an anguish that was delight and feverish need, she pushed against the leg that came between hers, seeking to ease the insistent ache at the pit of her stomach.

Instead the pressure sent her up in flames. She felt his face on her midriff, the heated kisses on her silken skin, and she writhed in an agony of pleasure.

The fire crackled softly, outlining his saturnine features as he efficiently stripped her and encouraged her to do the same to him, to run her hands over his taut frame, to familiarise herself with every inch of him.

Neither spoke; they had no need of words. There was no going back, no stopping. The sheepskin was soft and erotic against the sensitised skin of her back, her legs, as erotic as the hard male grace of the man poised over her.

She kissed the polished skin of his shoulder, tasted the faint film of salt, and then cried out a wordless exclamation as he gently forced an entry, made himself master of everything she had to give.

For a moment he froze, but her hands caught each other around his back, urging his lean hips down, and with a soft noise he pressed home into the slick, hot welcome. Fire shot through her, irradiating the flower of sensuality that bloomed deep within, and she found out that her body knew very well how to respond, arching into him, meeting the thrust of his loins with her feminine answer, wrapping her legs and arms around him to stop him from ever getting away.

Petra had no idea where this was heading, little understanding of the processes at work, but she knew that there was some destination, some place she was aimed for. The reaching, the yearning throbbed through her body, pushing her on, urging her upwards, and the promise was there, reliant on the hard possession of his body, but emanating from deep inside her...

And then she reached it, and the sounds she could hear were hers, the moans that sounded like torment, and in a way were. But he responded with the same choked gasps. Even as the waves of ecstasy rippled through her she opened her eyes a slit and saw his head thrown back, the devouring hunger tightening his features into a mask, impersonal, agonised, the muscles of his arms and shoulders cording with effort until he too reached the peak of his pleasure.

Then there was silence except for the crackle of the fire and the sounds of hurried breathing slowing as their hearts regulated. Petra lay in silky luxury, feeling the moisture dry on her skin except where he lay, loving him, loving the way his head rested against her breast.

He sighed and moved on to his side, scooping her up so that she was draped half over him. Still he said nothing. Dreamily she watched the flames in the fireplace, and slowly, imperceptibly the sweet pleasure of the moment was lost in a thought that popped up like a black wraith from her subconscious.

Was this what had driven her mother on her self-destructive path? Lost to everything but the need to reach that agonising rapture, time after time? Merciless shame came unbidden, forcing Petra to see herself abandoned, totally without morals, so lost to all that was right and decent that she had lain down on the floor for him.

Was he lying there despising her?

She bit her lip, wondering with a panic-stricken humiliation what she should do, when he said, 'Damn and blast and hell!'

Agony fountained through her. She twisted to look into his face, and saw—nothing. He was so adept at concealing his feelings that the autocratic lines and planes revealed nothing. The strange pale eyes were cool and impersonal, all heat and light gone.

She said in a flat little voice, 'I'm not sorry.'

'I am,' he muttered between his teeth as he got up and began to pull on his clothes. 'And so, princess, are you going to be when you realise what we've done.' His black brows drew together in a frown as he surveyed her slender body, its rosy flush of fulfilled passion fading. 'Get dressed, for God's sake!'

The whiplash flick to his tone brought her scrambling up to haul on her clothes with fingers that felt cold right down to the bones. Shame smeared across her warm and shining memories, dulling them, turning them into sordid recollections.

'I'll take you home,' he said in that level voice, not looking at her.

They hadn't been more than five unbearably silent minutes in the car when she blurted, 'You said that your parents rejected you. What did you mean?'

It seemed that the tension grated on him, too, for he answered readily but remotely, 'When I got old enough to be useful on the farm they stopped me from going across to the Andersons'. I had to milk before school and after; I was always tired, and you can imagine what that did to my school results. When the Andersons intervened my parents...sold me.'

'*What?*' She was scandalised, but each word that he said she hugged to her like a tiny unexpected present.

His mouth was a thin slash in the frightening hardness of his face. 'They made a deal. I could live with the Andersons if they made it worth my parents' while. So my parents got a permanent position in exchange for a son, and I was sent away to an accelerated boarding-school.'

Petra said in a shaken voice, 'That's barbaric.'

'It was the best thing that could have happened to me,' he said dismissively. 'Anyway, much the same happened to you, didn't it?'

Flinching, she shook an indignant head at the disbelieving look he flicked across her. 'No! My mother dumped me on Aunt Kath while she went for a holiday in Tahiti. But when it was time to give me back Uncle Laurence and Aunt Kath decided that I should stay with them. Why, I'll never know, because I was the most awful child, totally undisciplined. There was a court hearing, and they were awarded custody.'

The court case had been one of the scandals of the decade, with the details of her mother's affairs splashed through the newspapers for the delectation of avid readers. Too young to understand what it was all about, she had nevertheless been affected by it.

'Yes,' he said abruptly. 'It was a hell of a childhood. Did you know your father?'

'No. He left when I was only a baby, and died when I was just six.' She set her mouth. 'He was a lot older than my mother, almost fifty when I was born. He went overseas when he left us.'

Left one hell for another, mining for emeralds in some forsaken South American country. There he had died, having paid with his life for enough green crystals to set up a small trust fund for the daughter he had left behind. It would provide her with barely enough money to live on, but, as her aunt had explained, added to a salary it would buy her the pretty things she deserved.

Petra would rather have had a father.

Choosing the words carefully, she said, 'I couldn't have had kinder or more loving parents than Aunt Kath and Uncle Laurence. They were all that my own parents weren't able to be.'

The car swung into their entrance. Instead of driving straight in Caine stopped just inside the gate, and said in a harsh, thick voice, 'I didn't mean to hurt you, princess.'

It couldn't have been more plain that he was bidding her farewell.

Sobs ached in the back of her throat, but she managed to ask, 'Will you kiss me, please?'

He made a funny sound, half-laugh, half-groan, and reached for her.

His mouth was harsh, even cruel, taking hers as though he could never get enough of her. Somewhere deep inside her that flower bloomed again, a silky blossom of sensuality, the petals unfolding through her body. The hungry demand of his kiss reassured some basic, unregenerate part of her character. No matter what he said, what he did, he still wanted her as much as she wanted him.

Dragging in a deep breath, he tore his mouth free, and kissed her lashes, the curve of her cheekbone, pressing a last kiss at the corner of her mouth. 'If anything happens,' he muttered, 'if you get pregnant, tell me.'

Sheer panic swamped her mind. She didn't dare look at him in case he realised how shamefully afraid she was.

'Promise,' he demanded, his voice harsh and impeded, his mouth wonderfully gentle on her lashed eyes.

'Yes, I promise.' Her voice was shaky but definite.

He pulled away, and set the car in motion, jerkily pulling up under the *porte-cochère* to say savagely, 'Just get out and go, will you? Go, and don't look back.'

CHAPTER THREE

DESOLATION tore at her. Petra looked at him for one long moment, imprinting the bleak arrogance of his face on to her mind forever, then on an uncontrollable sob tore open the door and raced inside, almost colliding with her aunt.

With the sound of her startled voice ringing in her ears she ran up the stairs, tears falling as steadily as the rain.

'Darling, what on earth's happened?' Her aunt followed her in, her face horrified. 'Petra, dear——'

Petra didn't want to tell her, she just wanted to crawl into a hole somewhere and die, but she couldn't, she was going to have to live with this aching hole in her heart forever. Scrubbing at her eyes, she hiccuped, 'He said I'm too young—and I know—but I——'

'Oh, *darling*.'

Maternal arms enfolded her, held her close. She resisted, but after a moment their warmth was too much; she leaned her head on her aunt's shoulder and wept as though she was a small child once more, abandoning for grief and pain the control her aunt valued so highly.

'It's not the end of the world,' her aunt kept saying, just as she had promised through all the woes of childhood. 'I know it hurts, but it will get better. Never mind . . .'

Eventually exhaustion stopped Petra. Limp with reaction, she hiccuped, trying to control the long shudders that racked her body.

'That's better, poor baby. Have a bath,' her aunt advised, releasing her with a final hug, 'and I'll go down and get you a cup of tea. Do you want to tell me all about it?'

'It's over.' Petra essayed a smile, but failed lamentably. 'That's all.'

'It will seem better tomorrow,' the older woman averred. 'Hop into that bath, now.'

Petra managed the rest of the day reasonably well, even forcing down some dinner. Her uncle looked keenly at her but said nothing, eating his meal without much conversation, his expression set and difficult to read. After dinner he went out, and Petra climbed the weary stairs to bed, refusing the sedative her aunt wanted to give her.

She was still lying awake when her uncle came home, quite late. When she did drop off it was to a return of the explicit dreams that had plagued her these last weeks, but this time they were infinitely more disturbing, for this time she was no innocent, she knew what to expect, and in the heated eroticism of her memories she twisted and turned, burning all night for the weight of Caine's body, the ecstasy of his possession.

Drained, headachy, she woke to a softly weeping sky. It might have been appropriate, except that Petra's emotions were stormy, a turbulent mixture of anger and pain and grief and outrage.

'A rainy Sunday,' Aunt Kath said over breakfast, striving hard to lighten the atmosphere. 'We need it, of course; the garden was so dry I was going to water it today if it hadn't rained. Now, what shall we do?'

Petra knew that she had shocked and disappointed them both with her unbridled behaviour, was still disappointing them, and her love and respect made her look up with a determined attempt at interest.

'You and I are going to the Donaldsons',' Uncle Laurence reminded his wife, looking up from his toast.

'Are—oh, yes, of course, I'd forgotten.' Aunt Kath fluttered a little self-consciously before turning to Petra and asking solicitously, 'Darling, will you be all right by yourself?'

'Yes. Yes, of course I will.' She managed a smile, wobbly but definite, and saw them both relax a little. 'I'm sorry I've been so silly.' She was going to be by herself from now on, so she might as well get accustomed to it again.

But they had gone merely twenty minutes when there was a knock on the door. Petra almost didn't answer, until a second, imperative demand changed her mind. Hoping that her face was completely free from the effects of yesterday's firestorm of emotion, she opened the door.

Caine stood there, tall and dark and intimidating, his expression shuttered. 'Well,' he said curtly, when she hesitated, 'aren't you going to let me in?'

'Why? You said that it was over.'

He gave her a cool, considering glance, somehow raising her hackles. 'I've reconsidered,' he drawled. 'A good night's sleep convinced me that I was wrong.'

Colour flamed into her skin, then as quickly ebbed away. She pressed her lips together, and motioned him into the house, wondering confusedly why such a sophisticated man looked so—untamed in the cleverly decorated room.

Once in the sitting-room, she asked gravely, 'Why did you come, Caine?'

His mouth tightened, then relaxed into a cynical, almost taunting smile. 'To ask you to marry me,' he said.

Instincts she hadn't known she possessed warned her that something was wrong, something was very wrong, but even as she hesitated she saw the flicker of flame in his translucent eyes, and hope, not unmixed with a certain satisfaction, soared high again. He loved her, she was sure of it.

It was enough to ensure her capitulation.

A soaring wonder fired her expression to radiance. 'Aren't you supposed to kiss me when you ask me?' she said, smiling brilliantly through her tears.

Laughing deep in his throat, he locked her in the safe sanctuary of his arms, his mouth hard and demanding on hers. The familiar surge of passion engulfed her; she forgot her fears, forgot everything but her love and her need for him.

'I knew you couldn't leave me,' she whispered. 'Caine, I love you so much.'

He looked deep into her eyes, his own as clear as the pale sky of dawn, yet oddly bright—so bright that she couldn't see any emotion in them, nothing but the oddly cynical smile that didn't soften the hard line of his mouth. 'Do you, princess?' he asked softly. 'I hope you do.'

A month later they were wed at her local church, and after a small reception flew off to Thailand for three weeks.

Although during the short weeks of their engagement he had kissed her frequently, Caine had been completely controlled, not allowing the lightly teasing embraces to deepen into real passion. Petra thought she knew why, and was rather touched by his consideration. Ten days before their wedding she told him that there would be no baby.

'No?' he said, surveying her flushed face with the aloofness that was a part of his restraint.

'You sound a little disappointed.' Her voice was edged and jerky; since the first cramp the night before some frightened part of her had wondered whether he would use the fact that she wasn't pregnant to call off the wedding.

'No,' he said, but thoughtfully. 'Are you?'

Her colour deepened. 'No. Although later on I'd like to have your children.'

He raised his brows and smiled, watching her with the cool dispassion that he so often showed to her now. She knew that it was just because he was keeping such a tight rein on his desire, but sometimes his remoteness annoyed her so much that she wanted to smash through it and make him treat her as he had before, become the man she had fallen in love with.

But her aunt's training prevented such excessive behaviour. She, too, could practise restraint. She would show him that she was going to be a worthy wife. However, the weeks of self-discipline sharpened her appetite to such an extent that on their honeymoon she responded with open, adoring ardour, forgetting her insecurities in the bliss of his skilful, demanding lovemaking.

However, even drowned in rapture, so happy that she blossomed into beauty, Petra found that happiness had its limits. Although she loved him, and told him so often and with all her heart, he never said the same sweet words to her. She thrilled to his compliments—the words forced thickly from him during their lovemaking set fire to her blood—but the greatest prize of all, his avowal of love, was still out of her reach.

And he never again lost control as he had that first time. Indeed, he seemed to take pleasure in prolonging the delicious preliminaries until she was almost incoherent with passion before, with a smile that twisted his mouth, he would give her the ecstatic consummation she pleaded brokenly for. However much he appreciated her attempts to drive him out of his mind with her innocent, open sensuality, there was no repetition of the uncontrolled passion of that first time.

Some essential part of him was locked away, remote, impregnable.

But when she tried to tax him with the difference in him the cool crystals of his eyes warmed into the fire at the heart of a diamond, and all her doubts were lost in the flood of desire he summoned so easily from her.

Any fear that she was as much a slave to passion as her mother had been was ruthlessly proscribed, only sneaking back at odd times in the hot tropical nights when she listened to Caine's steady breathing, and caught herself thinking rather bleakly that she missed their communion in those first weeks.

Then he had treated her as another adult, discussing things with her, demanding that she use her brain; now she sometimes thought that he thought of her only as the delicious little sensualist he called her, the sexy nymph who always responded, no matter how tired she was, to the touch of his hand, the narrowed intent look that meant he was going to take her to bed. He was indulgent as to a much-loved child, and, although the hours they spent in each other's arms should have given her confidence, she sometimes thought she felt it draining away.

If only she hadn't succumbed so swiftly—but it seemed that she had no defences, no self-control where he was concerned. Perhaps if she had he might respect her a little more, and she wouldn't have this degrading feeling that she was now nothing more than a pretty toy.

But then, she thought as Auckland's harbours appeared in exquisite juxtaposition through the plane window, marriage needed compromise, periods of adjustment. Caine might still seem withdrawn, a little distant, but she had all the time in the world to discover the lights and shadows of his personality, and to win his respect.

Life as his wife proved every bit as exciting as she had fantasised. Quite often she accompanied her aunt to various social occasions that ranged from boring to fun, but the evenings were for Caine alone. Then the desire they kept at bay all day overflowed into passion. Periodically he suggested they go out, but when she protested that she would far rather be at home with him he agreed, a curious smile pulling at his mouth. Loving him more each day, Petra tumbled into his arms with a fresh passion each night, happy to be swept with him to that region where at last they became almost equals.

He put up with her attempts at housekeeping with a wry amusement, not even showing relief when she decided that for the present she would leave the running of the house to his very good daily woman, and agreeing that she should probably attend cooking lessons before she was let loose in the kitchen. So she went to a cordon bleu class for beginners, while dutifully heating the casseroles and vegetables that Mrs Sanderson prepared each day.

Two months after they were married, Caine came home one day a little early. After one look at the closed, saturnine mask of his face Petra asked anxiously, 'What's wrong?'

'I've just got the bill for your services.'

The savage inflexion in the deep voice trapped her astonished gaze. 'I don't know what you mean.'

He smiled, a set, savage twist to his mouth. 'I think you do, princess.' The word had always been an endearment, but now he made it an epithet, an obscenity. 'I've spent the last hour closeted with your uncle while he told me that I owe it to him—and to you—to lend him a large amount of money to put into that damned furniture factory he's been running into the ground for the past fifteen years.'

Bewildered and shocked by the repressed fury in his voice, the dark menace of his expression, Petra whispered, 'I don't know what you're talking about.'

He showed his teeth, making no attempt to hide his disbelief. 'Really? Come on now, Petra, you're not that stupid. You played your part in this sleazy con too well not to have known what was going on.'

Panic welled up through her, making her feel sick. Searching his face, she saw nothing but an icy, ugly contempt. Her mouth dried. Carefully she dampened her top lip with her tongue. 'I don't know,' she replied shakily, 'what you're talking about.'

He was watching her as though she was something small and loathsome, something he could scotch with his heel. 'Then let me refresh your memory. Not so very long ago your uncle finally realised that he was in such a mess that the only thing that would save his bacon was a quick injection of cash. Unfortunately, the bankers have seen this coming for the last ten years, and naturally enough refused to lend him the million or so dollars he needs to keep going—especially as he's notorious around the financial world as an inept manager. You said something?'

She bit her lip, shaking her head.

Still speaking in that cold, judicious tone, he resumed, 'So he looked around for some other way to get the money. And there was I, stupid enough to let him see that I found you attractive. You make very pretty bait, princess, and you were only too eager to help him, weren't you? But I had a few scruples; I imagine that they caused you some considerable irritation.'

'No,' Petra whispered, realising at last what he was getting at. 'Caine, it wasn't like that, I swear.'

'Don't try to lie your way out of it; he made it quite plain that you were in on the whole scheme.'

Furious that he should so misjudge her and Uncle Laurence, Petra grabbed his arm, gasping with shock and outrage when he shook her hand off as though it contaminated him.

'Don't touch me,' he said quietly, his brilliant eyes as cold as an antarctic iceberg. 'I should have been suspicious—but you were clever enough to fool me, you little slut. As soon as I decided there was no *honourable* way out, that the most *honourable* thing for me to do was end it, you did the only thing you could—seduced me with that virginal fire. Then you went home and told your loving uncle, so he could get out his shot-gun!'

Petra's horrified astonishment didn't impress him. His mouth thin and ruthless, he drawled, 'Surprising, when you think of it, that he trusted my honour that far. I know exactly what his opinion of me is. He's got more brains than I gave him credit for—he certainly picked the right man to con! I was easily persuaded. God, it was like going to bed with a houri—virginal and experienced at the same time, a kind of primitive, pristine temptress. I was furious with you and him, but I let my hormones do more of my thinking, and decided that he was right, you were no more knowing than a kitten with a ball of wool, and I owed it to you to marry you. A very *convenient* sense of honour, for both you and your uncle.'

Still shaking her head, Petra strove for a dignity she couldn't reach. She tried to speak, but her voice trembled so much that she couldn't get any words out.

'It was a nice little plot,' he said reflectively, watching her with icy disdain. 'He gets his million dollars, you get a man to sleep with, and your aunt can rest content that you're saved from following in your mother's far too embarrassing and public footsteps.'

She knew then. Something in the way he'd said 'your mother's footsteps' made her flinch as the realisation struck her like a bullet through the soul. He thought she was like her mother, a slave to the needs of her body. The desire she had revelled in, the honest expression of her love had disgusted him. An icy chill stole through her, reaching from her heart to her extremities, robbing her of intelligence, of everything but the blank darkness of shame. Slowly her lashes drooped, hiding eyes that were muddied and empty.

'You must think I'm an idiot,' Caine said in a voice tinged with soft menace. 'Which, of course, is exactly what I have been, led by the nose by a frantic little sensualist and her pimp of an uncle.'

Petra shuddered, but managed to say thinly, 'How dare you——?'

'Just how would you describe a man who sold his niece, however willing she was, to a man he distrusted and despised, so that he could keep his business going?'

'Uncle Laurence would never——' A sudden memory froze the words in her mouth. Like a ghost come back to haunt her, the overheard conversation between her uncle and aunt after her birthday party became horribly clear. She looked down at her hands, realising to her shock that she was wringing them, and that try as she did she couldn't still them.

'Yes,' he said silkily, watching those writhing hands with cruel, hard eyes. 'And you are a treacherous little whore, eager to hawk your favours to the highest bidder.'

Appalled, the colour washing from her skin, she flinched as though his words had been stones directed at her heart. Another memory struck her: the same word used with the same disgust by one of her mother's lovers, and her mother's tears, the undignified wailing and pleading, the attempts to justify herself.

The memory put steel in Petra's backbone; as her heart shivered into a thousand pieces she said blindly, 'If that's the way you think, there's nothing more to say.'

'No,' he replied, watching her with dead, cold eyes, 'except this—get out of here. I never want to see you again.'

CHAPTER FOUR

PETRA'S gaze was slightly unfocused as she sat down. There was a round of applause before Mrs Bracknell, the formidable chairperson for the Children's Fund, stood up, bestowing a gracious smile first on Petra, then around the room.

The applause wavered, and died. 'Thank you, Ms Stanhope, for that lucid account of our finances and your suggestions for next year,' she said, fixing a talkative woman with a frigid stare. The offender immediately hid behind her champagne-glass. Satisfied, Mrs Bracknell continued majestically, 'I know those who work in the office at the Children's Fund have found their lives much easier since Ms Stanhope joined us three years ago, to say nothing of the accountants who audit our books.' She smiled benignly at the spatter of laughter. 'Before Petra's arrival on the scene we were still an amateur organisation, doing good work but hampered by our lack of knowledge and direction. She has set up a system which has taken us into an entirely different region, one where we can really begin to see some results. She has also produced a scheme which should see us well on the way to our ultimate aim—the establishment of a Foundation that will help provide inexperienced parents with parenting skills, so that, in time, the Fund, which as you know helps mainly abused children, may be able to put itself out of a job.'

There was another polite round of applause. Petra looked around the restaurant, smiling slightly as she met the eyes of various women. The chairperson began again, her sonorous voice stopping the instant wave of conversation.

A slight throb in Petra's temple warned her of the imminence of a headache. This lunch was the sort of affair that bored her rigid, but she was confident that no sign of it appeared beneath the glossy shield of sophistication she had constructed so carefully to hide her emotions and her thoughts. And she wasn't expected to speak at every lunch; this was the half-yearly affair for the various committee members, and was more a social occasion than business. Which explained the expensive restaurant and the champagne ordered by many of the women.

Sure enough Mrs Bracknell soon finished, smiled around the room once more, and sat down, immediately turning to Petra to say, 'It's a pity Kath can't be here, dear, but I suppose she and Laurence are enjoying their Pacific cruise?'

'I had a letter from Aunt Kath yesterday, posted in Samoa. She says they're having a wonderful time, although Uncle Laurence's indigestion is still playing up a bit.'

'Ah, another three weeks will be good for both of them. Laurence has been looking quite tired these last few months. I'm sure the business is getting far too much for him. Why doesn't he give it up?'

Petra's thin shoulders moved in the slightest of shrugs. 'I think he likes keeping busy,' she remarked mildly.

Mrs Bracknell smiled, and patted her hand. 'Then why doesn't he let you take over the job for which you have trained yourself so well?' she said, using her position as an old friend of the family quite shamelessly. 'You've done wonders with us, dragging our piddling little charity kicking and screaming into the twentieth century, but there's really not a lot left for you to do, is there? Oh, we'll be eternally grateful if you stay on, but you're beginning to look as though you'd like a new challenge. And the logical place to go is Stanhope's.'

Petra's expression didn't change, but she allowed a gleam of irony to show beneath her lashes. It was impossible to put Mrs Bracknell in her place, or to hide anything from her. 'You know Uncle Laurence,' she said, concealing her frustration with her lovely, serene smile. 'He's never accustomed himself to women in positions of responsibility, let alone power.'

The older woman clucked her tongue. 'Then it's time he learned,' she declared robustly. 'It's a real waste. You have your Commerce degree, and that difficult Management qualification, and, heaven knows, you couldn't do any——' She stopped, then sighed. 'Well, poor old Laurence has never really been a businessman,' she finished with unusual abruptness. 'It's time he gave up.'

'I think this cruise is a hopeful sign,' Petra said gently. 'It's the first time ever that he's let Aunt Kath coax him away for more than three weeks at a time.'

'I certainly hope so.' Her inquisitor was silent for a moment, then asked, 'Are you going to the Easter Racing Carnival this weekend?'

Petra braced herself. 'I hadn't planned to.'

'But you will, won't you, and go in for the best-dressed woman there?' Mrs Bracknell patted her hand. 'It netted us quite a lot of money when you won last year and put the prize up for auction. And we couldn't have bought the publicity.'

Sighing, Petra resigned herself to the inevitable. She had hated it, people staring at her, cameras, hype—she had felt stripped and displayed naked for everyone to see. But the older woman was right; her action had given the Fund a lot of very valuable publicity. 'Yes, all right.'

'Good girl.' Mrs Bracknell beamed at her, those shrewd eyes resting a moment on the still, calm face with a perspicacity that made Petra shrink back a little.

The lunch wore on. Petra's temple began to throb in earnest, so a few minutes before the end she murmured an excuse and slipped away into the cloakroom, whistling silently as she saw the size of it. Clearly the restaurant owners had spared no expense in any of the fittings. Cooled by a faintly humming air-conditioner, the room was outfitted as a very opulent retiring-room, brilliant lighting reflecting back from a mirrored wall so that the most meticulous woman could do a perfect repair to her make-up.

Frowning at the glare, Petra ran a glass of water, and wandered around the corner. There, in a blessedly dim, cool alcove hidden from the rest of the room was a leather sofa and two armchairs. Thankfully, she sat down and fossicked in her bag for a painkiller. Headaches were rare for her, but they were usually ferocious if they managed to get a hold, and she wanted to nip this one in the bud because she and David were going to the theatre that night.

Eyes closed, she leaned back, relaxing the taut muscles at the back of her neck. Her long hands lay loosely in her lap, the softly buffed nails pink with health, her only jewellery a rose diamond ring that had belonged to her grandmother Stanhope on her right hand. Along with his surname, she had given up wearing a wedding-ring when Caine left her. Her marriage had been a sham, and she was too proud to pretend otherwise.

She had learnt not to try to block her memories; if she managed it they sneaked into her dreams. So she sat quietly, her face composed and still while the air-conditioner hummed softly, her full mouth held in its normal rigid discipline, so normal now that probably no one realised how soft and reckless it could be. Had once been, when she was too young to understand that wantonness ran in her blood.

Slowly the pain, both mental and physical, receded into blessed numbness. She was just about to get up and go back to the room when the door into the restaurant slammed open, bringing with it laughter and the conflicting scents of at least two women.

'...such a snotty, stuck-up bitch.' That was Tracey Porter, whose husband had made a quick fortune in computer software, and who saw charity work as the best way to crash Auckland's society. 'No wonder they call her the Stone Princess.'

Petra's heavy eyelids lifted. She was just about to get to her feet when the other woman gurgled, 'It's rather a clever play on words, isn't it? Petra means stone or rock or something, doesn't it?'

Indecision kept Petra still for just too long. Tracey Porter said eagerly, 'I heard the other day that she's been married. I wouldn't have thought she had enough red blood in her to want to go to bed with a man.'

There was no way she could get out without making a fuss. Petra stuck her fingers in her ears, but both women had drunk enough champagne to lift their voices, and she could still hear most of what they said.

'...put her off men well and truly.'

'But what about David Carey?'

The second woman ran some water, and shouted above it, 'I'm not saying they don't go to bed together now and then, but I think they're more old friends than lovers.'

'What about her husband, then? What was he like?'

Petra sat frozen with anger and distaste. The second woman was Johnny Donaldson's wife, a couple of years younger than Petra, and until that moment she had thought they were friends.

'Caine? Oh, God, he was to die for. Ab-so-lute-ly gorgeous, tall and dark and striking, mean, moody and magnificent, with the kind of throw-away sadism that appeals to the masochist in every woman, and a mouth that promised the delights of paradise—well, perhaps not, the delights of the devil might be a better way of putting it. He'd been Jan Brewster's lover before he met Petra, and she damn near cut her wrists when he dumped her. Even though she's married now Jan still sighs when she thinks of him. She told me once that he was the most fantastic lover she'd ever had, so inventive and with such *stamina*.'

She invested the words with a slow, salacious pleasure that set Tracey laughing wickedly. 'Who was this paragon, for heaven's sake? Where is he? Within reach?'

The coppery taste of nausea filled Petra's mouth. Breathing deeply, she pushed her fingers harder across her ears, striving to shut out the intrusive voices, and failing.

'He's Caine Fleming,' Sophie Donaldson said. 'They broke up after a month or so of marriage—no one knows why 'cause Petra isn't telling—and Caine took himself off to America, where he found a computer firm started by a mad scientist who had no idea how to market the fruits of his genius. Caine bought him out, bunged him back in the lab where he's gone on to produce better and better computers, and turned the firm into Patience Computers.'

'My God!' Tracey's astonishment made Petra wince and belatedly wriggle her fingers to block their words, even if she couldn't shut out their voices. However, she heard her squeal, 'The billionaire? Why——' before it worked.

Her headache had come back in full force by the time they left, and as the last thing she wanted was for them to realise that she had overheard them she had to stay in the room until the end of the luncheon, when a crowd of women came in and she was able to escape in their midst.

But, although back at the office she managed to kill the headache, and even produce some work during the rest of the afternoon, when she got home she took off the superbly cut cool wool suit with its fashionable short straight skirt and classic collarless jacket, eased off shoes and tights in exactly the same colour, and stood for a few minutes in the dressing-room off her cream bedroom looking at herself in the mirror, the mask of her control for once abandoned.

Even her soft blue satin petticoat and French knickers couldn't lend much overt sensuality to her body, she thought, eyeing her slight breasts and handspan waist. That violent, unrestrained passion was well hidden, thank God.

What on earth had Caine seen in her, eight years ago? The esoteric pleasure of initiating a virgin, she supposed. The destruction of innocence? As callow as they came, she had been startlingly naïve. To a man ten years her senior she must have been green indeed.

Perhaps it served him right that instead of the shrinking virgin he no doubt expected he got her mother's daughter. Because that was when he had changed. It was after they had made love that first time that she'd noticed the difference in him, the subtle withdrawal, the carefully hidden distaste, but she had been too ingenuous to realise the reason for it.

If Caine had married her for her innocence he must have been badly shocked when the taint in her blood had surfaced. Had he wondered whether he had married a nymphomaniac? *Like mother, like daughter?* Naturally, he had taken the first opportunity he found to end their marriage. Aunt Kath had always told her that men liked to be the pursuers, that they preferred their women pure, needing to be wooed and romanced into sex, and Aunt Kath had been right.

Petra, of all people, should have known just how men reacted to open hunger. Her mother's lovers had always eventually been repelled by the unashamed carnality of her appetites. She clamped her lips together, remembering how her mother had embarrassed everyone with her tears and her temper, the clinging notoriety of her love affairs and the public quarrels, and the even more public reconciliations.

Even now when Anne Stanhope's name was mentioned there was a certain smile that men used, a certain speculative note in their voices that sickened Petra and shamed her. It extended to her, too; she had learned to freeze off men who tried with sly insinuations and hints to discover whether she was prey to the same demons as her mother, at the mercy of every fleeting need, every passing passion.

Colour slowly faded from Petra's skin. She pulled the slides from her dark blonde hair, and let it flow free down her back, shaking it a little to ease her tense scalp. Looking down at her slender body, her mouth tightened in disgust at the aching presence of desire. Even after all these years she still wanted Caine. The thought was a bitter taste in her mouth.

For the loan he had been so incensed about had been an excuse. In the dreadful days after Caine had left for America she had asked her uncle what had happened, and he had told her that yes, he had insisted Caine marry her; it was, he said gruffly, with angry embarrassment, the only honourable thing for him to do after he had seduced her.

'But you didn't know,' she protested.

His eyes had slid past hers. 'Your aunt knew,' he said shortly.

She bit her lip. Of course it wouldn't have taken much deduction for Aunt Kath to realise what had happened.

'What about the money?'

'Damned cad, he had no right to worry you about——'

'Did you borrow from him?'

Startled by her persistence, he gave her a narrow look, but she met it with determination. He didn't think women should have to bother their pretty little heads about the sordid realities of life, but this was important; she had to know.

'Yes,' he admitted reluctantly, walking across to stare out of the window. 'I asked him for a loan, and he gave it to me, but it is bridging finance only. I have organised another loan from the bank.'

It was like a death-blow. But she persevered. 'He said that—you told him I knew what you were doing.' Colour stained her cheeks, then ebbed, leaving her regular, unspectacular features as pale as they had been in the moonlight the first night they'd met, she and Caine.

Her uncle muttered something beneath his breath. 'Petra, don't. You're well rid of him, he was not our sort, it's as well he showed his true colours before there were any children. You'll get over him; this will soon be just an unpleasant memory. I thought you and your aunt might like to go to England——'

'Did you tell him I knew about it, Uncle Laurence?'

'Why?' her uncle said explosively. 'Why would I say a thing like that?'

Why, indeed? So Caine had lied to her. If his reason for leaving had been the loan, and what he assumed to be her part in securing it, then when he realised he was wrong he would have come back. If he had loved her. But then, he had never loved her.

Petra's mouth compressed into a tight smile, cynicism and sadness inextricably mixed. He had used the loan to cover up his real reason for leaving her, which was that she disgusted him.

Nice try, Caine, but it hadn't worked. Oh, how she must have sickened him with her wantonness, her demands, her blatant appreciation of his lean body and the magical sensations he gave her, her gasps and sobs and writhing when he touched her, the whole lustful earthiness of her response. She had sensed his withdrawal, but had not known how to deal with it, and in the end he had been forced to be cruel to disentangle himself from her.

At least when the inherited weakness appeared it had been only for one man, and she had learnt her lesson. She was definitely mistress of her emotions and her appetites now. No man would ever have her at a disadvantage again. That had become her creed and her ambition, and for the last eight years she had carefully built her walls and stocked her garrison until she believed that she had attained her goal.

Smiling sadly, she showered, thrusting Caine Fleming and the mistakes of her youth far behind her where they belonged. The present was trying to convince her uncle to let her work for Stanhope Ltd, and a life that was busy and satisfying enough in its own way, with David Carey as a friend she could rely on.

Not as a lover, not even occasionally.

CHAPTER FIVE

EASTER turned out to be a rare time of fine weather and sunshine, ideal for the Racing Carnival. The temperatures were kind and summery, so Petra wore a crêpe suit in a clear periwinkle blue that transformed her eyes into that exact colour. Not brand new, it was one of her favourites. The asymmetrically pleated jacket had a deep keyhole neckline emphasised by a pinky gold brooch of her grandmother's, its tassel hanging seductively to make the most of the hint of cleavage that was all she possessed. She hoped fervently that the weather wouldn't get too hot, because the long, tightly fitted sleeves were going to be profoundly uncomfortable if it did.

With it she wore a draped hat that hid her muted ash-blonde hair completely, and shoes and bag all of the same colour as the suit. Discreet rose gold earrings and a light mist of Ivoire perfume completed the outfit.

'There,' she said cynically to her reflection, 'the armour is complete.'

Since David was spending the weekend in Australia, she went alone, but she knew almost everyone there, and within minutes of her arrival was busy acknowledging greetings, and talking. She even managed to be affable to Tracey Porter and her big bear of a husband.

Behind the armour of her cosmetics and clothes and excellent manners, deep, deep down where her wild emotions roamed unconfined Petra was angry and hurt, but common sense told her that eavesdroppers never heard good of themselves. And, for all that Tracey possessed a taste for malice that might get her into trouble one day, she was merely a rather foolish woman.

Before long boredom crept over Petra, dulling the sparkling day, making the crowds of people seem garish and loud, their smiles too wide, their clothes worn to shock or impress. She strove against the tedium, a little worried because boredom seemed to be assuming a more prominent place in her life than it should. Surely she was not so spoiled that she became like so many favoured people, unable to find challenges enough to make life worthwhile?

As she smiled and chatted and circulated she decided that she was going to stop hesitating. The Children's Fund no longer needed her, so she would find a way to work at Stanhope's, Uncle Laurence and his outmoded prejudices notwithstanding.

Much to her surprise and irritation she was chosen for the line-up in the contest. It was when she was standing in front of cameras and people, chin lifted, an enigmatic little smile curling her rigidly disciplined mouth, silently hating all the eyes on her that she saw a man standing with his head held arrogantly in a manner she had never forgotten.

Also recognisable was the dark wavy hair, and the wide shoulders—farmer's shoulders—she had teased him once. And the crystalline intensity of the stare; Caine had always made her feel that when she was within sight he saw nothing else.

The people, the horses, the close-cut grass, the flowers, and the buildings whirled for a hideous moment, then righted themselves. Behind skilfully applied cosmetics the colour drained from her skin.

Her lashes trembled; through the tumult she heard another woman's name called, and realised to her intense relief that she had not won. The smile wavered on her lips as cameras flashed and the crowd clapped. Very carefully she avoided looking in one particular direction, but when it was over she allowed herself a small terrified peep.

A sigh of relief hurt her lungs. There was no sign of him—no tall, vital man with an imperious, mocking face and eyes so cold they could freeze the marrow in your bones.

Turning blindly away, she cannoned into Tracey Porter. 'Sorry,' she said, well aware of the curious eyes that searched her pale face.

'You look as though you've had a shock!'

'I've got a headache.' It was the first thing that came into her mind.

'Oh, what *bad* luck,' Tracey commiserated fulsomely.

'Isn't it?' There was a fine trace of irony in Petra's tone that went straight past the woman, who was watching her with something unhealthily avid in her glance. 'I'll head off for home, I think.'

'What a pity. Look, I've got painkillers in my bag; why don't you take one and have a cup of tea, and——?'

Petra was cross with herself for being immediately suspicious when the woman was just trying to be kind. It took an effort, but she produced a pale smile as she said politely, 'No, I think I'll go, thank you, Tracey.'

Swiftly she walked away through the throngs of well-dressed people, the sunlight, the noise and the laughter, and out into the members' car park.

A voice from behind called, 'Petra.'

She put her hand out and caught the side mirror of a car, using it as a support while her heart thundered painfully in her chest.

'You saw me,' Caine said, his cool, curt intonation not altered a whit by the eight years he had spent in America.

Dragging in a deep breath, she turned to face him, her lashes hiding her thoughts, her mouth controlled and straight. 'I thought I did,' she admitted, keeping her gaze firmly fixed on his face. 'But when I looked again you weren't there, so I concluded I'd been mistaken.'

A narrow smile creased his cheeks, but his eyes were coolly watchful, assessing just how his appearance was affecting her. Petra's back stiffened. So automatically that she didn't realise she was doing it, she lifted her chin. Caine's smile hardened.

He looked his thirty-six years, the inborn charisma qualified now by an added depth, a maturity that increased his potent male attraction. There was something about the arrangement of his features, the straight blade of his nose and the startling transparence of his eyes, something about the golden-brown skin and wide high forehead, something about the autocratic line of jaw and cheekbone that attracted women's eyes, and would until the day he died.

Basic animal magnetism, Petra thought snidely.

She had fallen for it when she was eighteen, and she felt it now, but hard work and discipline in the intervening eight years had given her a poise that wasn't easily upset by a primal mating-signal.

'So what are you doing here?' she asked in her easiest social voice.

'You sound just like your aunt.'

Her brows lifted. She allowed the tiniest bit of disdain to appear for a micro-second in her expression. 'Really?' she said, and turned away.

'Where are you going?'

Yes, that was more like it, that had the authentic crack of the whip.

'Back to my car. I'm getting rather hot, and people are staring.'

'That causes you problems?' he asked ironically. 'You certainly weren't averse to parading yourself for the delectation of most of New Zealand a few minutes ago. I noticed the television cameras lingering over you with slavering interest. You should have won, incidentally.'

Refusing to defend herself, she shrugged. If she told him that her 'parading' had been done for abused children he would laugh. And disbelieve her. Eight years ago, when a selfish adolescent, she had not been interested in those less fortunate than herself.

A cheerful crowd of people wandered past, a family party whose laughter and teasing remarks fell pleasantly through the warm, clear air as they went towards their vehicles. Petra noticed the women's eyes linger on Caine's tall figure, elegant, whipcord-lean in the dark lounge-suit that hugged his wide shoulders and narrow hips, moulded perfectly to the heavy muscles in his thighs.

Animal magnetism, she reminded herself curtly, wondering why such primitive sexuality was enhanced by civilised and expensive tailoring.

With fervent gratitude she recognised the silver shape of her car. Shock had flayed her emotions raw, as though she had been pilloried for the express amusement of everyone who saw her.

'Nothing to say for yourself?' he needled, when the group had passed them.

'No.' She looked at him steadily, her gaze opaque and carefully serene. 'The day you left I decided I would never make excuses to a man again.' She showed perfect teeth in a small, mirthless smile. 'It's a vow I've managed to keep.'

His eyebrows lifted in taunting enquiry, and she was assailed by the uncomfortable suspicion that she should not have said that. He was too astute, able to string apparently disconnected facts together with alarming flashes of intuition that took him far beyond the logical processes of his brilliant mind.

'I don't recollect you making any excuses then,' he observed neutrally. 'No excuses, no explanations. You just packed up and left.'

'You were definitely not in the mood for believing anything I said. So what *are* you doing here?' she asked again, distracting him with the question, her voice as indifferent as she could make it. She had no intention of talking over that last searing scene.

'I came to see you, of course.'

For a moment hope, wild as the storm, raced through Petra, knocking her hard-won control awry. But before it had time to fully register she realised that he had said only that he'd come to *see* her.

It took her an effort of will to regain her composure, but she managed to do it, even to say in an aloof little voice, 'Really? Why?'

'Perhaps it was just to see what sort of person you've grown up to be,' he told her with casual brutality.

'Well, now you've seen you can go back to America and your empire,' she said smoothly, stopping as they came up to her car. She didn't allow her relief to show, but merely turned to him with the slight, meaningless smile she had perfected over the years, and surveyed him with cool, flat blue eyes, missing nothing, revealing nothing.

He looked totally at home. Although Caine had grown up on a back-country farm he possessed an autocratic confidence that made him accepted wherever he was. It was in-built, that effortless authority, but his years of power had honed it to an instrument of intimidation.

Petra inserted her car key into the lock.

His black brows snapped together. 'What on earth have you done to yourself? You were a docile little girl when we were married, obedient enough to let your aunt and uncle talk you into marrying a man you didn't love, but at least you had some spark, some fire. Now you're like a beautiful puppet. I watched you parading in front of the eager eyes of men out there, and none of it touched you, did it? None of the lust and the avidity and the sly surmises. They slid down over the glossy shell and landed at your pretty feet, and you walked over them all, untouched by the dirt and the heat and the desire. What the hell have you done to yourself?'

The intensity of his words ate into the armour of her composure like acid into steel. Mesmerised by the crystal transparence of his gaze, she shook her head, unable to answer such a direct attack.

'Oh, get into the car!' he demanded savagely. 'I'll follow you home.'

Frowning, her voice losing a little of its brittle steadiness, she said, 'I don't want—that is, you're not coming home with me.'

'Of course I am,' he replied calmly. 'Get in, you look silly standing there with your mouth open. It doesn't go with the fashion-plate image.'

Of course her mouth wasn't open, as she discovered when she tried to close it. Her grip of the situation began to melt through her hands, carrying away with it her confidence and poise. 'Caine, you are not coming home with me,' she said clearly, decisively, a bite in her tone.

He grinned and leaned down to within an inch of her face, holding her captive with the lazy insolence of his smile. 'How,' he invited, 'are you going to stop me, Miss Cool and Mighty?'

To which, of course, there was no answer. The tip of her tongue stole out to dampen dry lips. In a husky voice she said, 'I can't. But I can stop you from coming inside.'

Something smouldered in the depths of his amazing eyes. 'Sooner or later you'd get sick of dodging me, so you might as well let me say what I want to say,' he pointed out as he straightened up. 'Anyway, I need some information from you.'

She took the opportunity to slide into the car, but although she put the key in the starter she didn't turn it. Instead she looked up with a bewildered frown. 'I don't know what you're talking about.'

'You'll find out soon enough.' He stood back and said, 'Drive carefully. The traffic's bedlam out there.'

'After America you can say the traffic's bad?'

'American roads are geared for bedlam,' he told her. 'These are not. On your way, princess.'

Stupid, bewildering tears widened her eyes. With an inelegant sniff she set the Volvo in motion, wondering dismally why a simple word, one he had used as both an endearment and a curse, had the power to move her so unbearably.

He was already waiting for her when she drove into her garage, his elegant figure disposed bonelessly against the wall by her front door, coat and tie removed to reveal an ivory silk shirt. A study in masculine grace, but with the implication of strength and power in his loose-limbed stance and carriage. The matching jacket and trousers suited him, as did the jeans, leather and suede which she was more used to seeing him in. He was able to go from country casual to city formal just as easily as he had come from that small farm in the King Country to lead a multi-million dollar corporation in the cut-throat world of international computing.

Ignoring him, Petra collected her wits for the encounter ahead, noting the anonymous BMW parked beneath the huge jacaranda tree that graced her front garden. On the way home she had decided that she would gain nothing by refusing to let him in; she might as well see what he wanted so that it would be over and done with.

The sound of her heels tap-tapping on the path followed her up to the entrance. Her house was an old-fashioned two-storey cottage in the suburb of Remuera—a dress-circle location with a superb view out across the intervening ridges and valleys to the harbour, and, beyond, in the dim blue distance, the beginning of the long northern peninsula that pointed over two hundred miles up into the green Pacific Ocean.

Straightening up, Caine watched her arrive, his face as expressionless as she hoped hers was.

'Do your eyes still change colour with whatever you wear?' he astounded her by asking.

She lifted her brows. 'I think so,' she answered imperturbably, readying the house-key. 'They always have.'

With cool effrontery he took the key from her hand and opened the door, then stood back to let her through. Stiffly, she preceded him inside, hating the fact that he was there. This house was her sanctuary, the only place where she could really relax.

'This looks very "English country",' Caine said, gazing around with open interest. 'Pleasantly shabby. How long have you lived here?'

'A couple of years,' she told him, her tranquil tone belying her emotions.

'Where did you live before that?'

Tension prickled across her skin as she said, 'With Aunt Kath and Uncle Laurence.'

His mouth tightened. 'So devoted,' he gibed. 'How on earth did you manage to tear yourself away from those loving, possessive arms?'

'Easily enough.' Which was a lie. When their marriage had broken up she had returned to her aunt and uncle with all the inevitability of a pigeon finding its way back to the one loft it called home, and she had lived there happily enough until she had seen the house, badly in need of renovation, but irresistible.

Her mother had just died, leaving Petra enough to buy the place. For some weeks she had dithered between giving the money to charity and using it to buy the house, but in the end her first instinct won. She had donated her mother's estate to a research laboratory that was doing research on alcoholism, and negotiated a loan from the bank to buy the house. With very little to spend on repairs, she had left the bottom storey as it was, using what spare money she had to renovate the upstairs part.

It had been difficult, but she had persisted in her decision to live there until she had managed to get her aunt and uncle to accept the idea with resignation, if not approval.

'Perhaps you're growing up at last.' He frowned at a large painting of a cloudbank, smooth and sophisticated, the only sign of life in the whole big canvas a small totara tree silhouetted against the horizon. It was an impressive piece, stark with the simplicity of good art.

'I like that,' he said, surprising her because he was a connoisseur, and she had bought the painting simply because it appealed to her. Something in the lonely durability of that small tree against the immense impersonality of the sky comforted her, although to others it seemed cold and empty.

'Caine, what do you want?' She had to ask because the sight of him pacing through her rooms with the athletic grace of a predator made her uneasy.

'You know what I want.'

For a moment she felt a return of that flare of hope, but she doused it brutally. The expression on his lean face told her that he certainly didn't want her.

His brows lifted in sardonic appreciation of her confusion, but he went on evenly, 'I want the million dollars your uncle Laurence borrowed from me to keep his factory going.'

This time her mouth did drop. Petra felt it fall as she stared foolishly at him, her lashes stretched open to their widest extent. He was cynically amused at her reaction, those impossible eyes as sharp as shards of diamond.

'You'd better sit down,' he suggested laconically. 'I gather from the stunned stare that your adored uncle Laurence didn't tell you about this part of the deal.'

'I—no. No. I thought——' She touched her tongue to her parched lips, noting vaguely that he responded with a narrow-eyed stare as though he suspected her of trying to influence him.

Making no attempt to hide the aggression in his voice, Caine stated, 'But you knew that your uncle bartered you for the money he needed. I got your style and breeding and a back-door access to the upper-class. You were only too eager to help him out, as I remember. One thing I can't fault is your loyalty to the people who brought you up.'

'But Uncle Laurence said...' she muttered, shaking her head. 'He told me it was just a bridging loan, that he'd covered it with a loan from the bank.'

His lip curled. 'He lied. He'd already tried the banks and been turned down. I damned near laughed in his face myself, but because he was your uncle I lent him the money. Which is now due.'

Petra pressed her cold hands to her clammy cheeks, for the third time that day terrified she was going to faint. In an instant she was jerked from her position just inside the door, and thrust into a chair.

'Put your head between your knees,' the crisp, impersonal voice advised, but, when she shivered, unable to move, Caine's lean fingers found the nape of her neck and thrust her head down.

It helped. The monstrous whirling stopped, although her stomach still lurched with nausea. However, the sound of his footsteps dragged her eyelids up; he was rummaging in the sideboard. Even as she began to protest he made a small triumphant sound, and poured brandy from a decanter into a glass.

A few seconds later it was held to her lips. 'Drink up,' he commanded, and obediently she swallowed, shuddering as the smooth golden liquid slid down her throat. After the first mouthful she shook her head, but he ordered implacably, 'Finish it,' and she did.

'Yes,' he said, the words coldly sarcastic, 'your surrogate parents trained you well, didn't they? You respond immediately to a direct order.'

Her eyes widened endlessly as they were trapped by the cold transparence of his. Sudden colour blazed like a beacon in her translucent skin. She choked on the last drop of brandy, and by the time she had mopped herself up she had managed to thrust her memories back into the dark recesses of her mind where they belonged, bitter nuggets of humiliation from the most humiliating period of her life.

Striving for the detachment she had worked so hard to attain, Petra said aloofly, 'So you expect me to believe that my uncle s-sold me in return for the loan of a million dollars? A million dollars that he hasn't repaid?'

Caine gave a short, humourless laugh. 'I have to admire you for your determination to keep up this charade. Come on now, Petra, I didn't fall for that sweet, wide-eyed innocence eight years ago, and I've grown a lot tougher since then. Why in the name of God do you think I left you? I was furious to find out you had sold yourself to me.'

'I didn't! I knew nothing about his plans, or even that Stanhope's was in trouble—if it was,' she added defiantly.

'Oh, it was—still is, for that matter. He's done exactly what I guessed he'd do—used the money to pay off the most urgent loans, but taken no steps to put the factory's finances on to a better footing.'

She drew in a deep, ragged breath. 'Even if that's so, I knew nothing about it.' Something acid and unregenerate prompted her to add, 'And you needn't lie—I know exactly why you left me.'

'Indeed?' he said silkily. 'Why, if it wasn't the fact that if I'd wanted to buy a wife I'd certainly have preferred to have chosen her myself?'

Her eyes fell. 'I—well, I bored you,' she said in a muffled voice. It was too humiliating to tell him that she knew he'd been sickened by her clinging demands, her open sensuality.

'Bored me? Hardly. Until I found out why you married me I was happy enough with our marriage,' he said in a lethal monotone, letting his eyes drift down over her body in an insulting, sexual survey that told her exactly what he was referring to. 'Not that I enjoyed being forced into it, but I told myself that you were only a kid, too young to know what you'd done. I was a fool. I've heard of arranged marriages, even seen a few of them, but by and large both parties knew what they were getting into. What really stuck in my craw was being taken for a ride by a nubile little sensualist and her greedy uncle.'

Wounded to the soul by the cold contempt of his gaze, the crisp even voice saying words that tore her heart with their barbs, Petra said beneath her breath, 'I—no. I—it wasn't like that.'

'Can you deny that Laurence pushed us together—in spite of the fact that he despised everything I stood for?'

Wearily she shook her head. 'But I——'

'And can you deny that he more or less held a shotgun at my head, demanding that I marry you?'

'No,' she said in muffled tones, shame eating at her. 'I know he did—he admitted it after you'd gone. But I didn't tell him that we—what had happened. Aunt Kath guessed.'

He lifted his eyebrows. 'Really? She's psychic, is she? You'll forgive me, I'm sure, if I find that impossible to believe.'

Light suddenly dawned. Petra stared at him, indignation breaking through the rigid constraint she had imposed on her expression. 'You mean you think it was a set-up—that I . . . let you make love to me so you'd have to marry me, just so Uncle Laurence could ask you for money?'

His shoulders moved in a shrug that drew attention to the sleek swell of muscle beneath the ivory silk. '*Let* me make love to you?' he drawled. 'It seemed to me that when you realised that I was serious about no longer seeing you you set about seducing me with all the aplomb of a much more experienced woman. Perhaps you learned more from your mother than you realised.'

'No!' she blurted, horrified, sickened.

He lifted a cynical brow. 'It's been done often enough, princess. Whatever . . .' He didn't raise his voice, but she subsided into silence, her hot protest dying unspoken under his merciless gaze. 'Your uncle had a pigeon for plucking. And I, poor besotted fool that I was, was prepared to lend the money to him. Even though I knew he was probably about the least efficient businessman I'd ever come across. You adored him, and that was enough for me. It wasn't until everything was signed and sealed that he let slip that you knew exactly what you were doing—and why.'

'No,' she whispered, shaking her head.

But he was just as he had been that awful day when her life had shattered around her—icily angry, totally unreasonable, lost in a rage so intense that she had been beaten to the ground before its onslaught. Before she had time to realise what she was doing she shrank away from him.

'Oh, for God's sake!' he exclaimed disgustedly. 'At least admit, Petra, that normally there is no way your very patrician relatives would have let me anywhere near you, their adored little princess, carefully reared to adorn some man's castle, some man of "breeding" and "birth".'

Even after all these years she could hear her uncle's intonation in his savage voice.

Petra said hopelessly, 'I loved you.'

'That wasn't love,' he sneered. 'That was sex. You were hot for it, so your uncle provided you with a playmate. Perhaps he thought that as well as bailing him temporarily out of trouble a husband might forestall any embarrassing affairs—like your mother's.'

All colour drained from her skin. Cold beads of sweat sprang out across her upper lip and at her temples. It was one thing to suspect that her unrestrained ardour was the real reason for his leaving, it was another to have it confirmed so matter-of-factly.

'However, that's all water under the bridge,' he continued, apparently not noticing. 'All I want is to find out how your uncle means to repay his debt to me.'

'I don't know,' she said, admitting at last that she believed him, and cold with disillusion because, if her uncle had lied to her, then he could have lied to Caine, too. But why would he have said that she was part of the plot, if plot it had been?

'No, I don't suppose you do,' he sneered. 'He doesn't get much backing from his women, does he, poor devil?

You and his wife spend the money while he schemes and blackmails for it...'

Petra's control snapped. Before she did anything stupid like scream at him or burst into tears as her mother had used to do she had to get rid of him. Lurching to her feet, she said in a low, trembling voice, 'He's not here. He's on a cruise around the Pacific. Will you please go? *Just go.* Get the hell out of here!'

'What a *convenient* time for him to be away. All right, I'm going—for the present.' His taunting smile didn't soften the threat of the last three words. 'I rather like the first faint sign of animation, incidentally. You look more like the girl I married. She wasn't exactly adult, but she showed some signs of getting there. And she was vibrant with life and passion. If I'd known that your only ambition in life was to emulate a stuffed doll I might have taken you with me when I left for America.'

'I wouldn't have gone to the end of the road with you!' Petra snapped, stung to the quick.

Caine grinned insolently. 'All I'd have needed to do was kiss you, and you'd have followed me barefoot across the world,' he said, watching as her skin coloured in a fiery flood.

'Get out!' she shouted, and, laughing, he left her. A moment later she heard his car purring out on to the street.

Still shaking, and nauseated by the faint taste of brandy in her mouth, she raced up the stairs, skidding to a stop in the middle of her bedroom, a hand clenched over her heart.

As she looked around at the elegant room, French to its ceiling with a magnificent walnut bed inlaid with mother-of-pearl that had come from her great-grandmother's house, its turn-of-the-century opulence emphasised by soft winter-white furnishings, she thought with a rather desperate relief that at least he hadn't seen this. It was a dead give-away that beneath the cool objectivity of her façade there lurked a closet romantic.

Mechanically she stripped off, carrying her clothes to the dressing-room that occupied what had been the second bedroom. Then she cleaned her teeth and showered, and creamed the skilfully applied make-up from her face, as always feeling that she had removed a disguise.

It invariably surprised her that she looked younger with her face bare; more, she thought with something suspiciously like a sob, like the schoolgirl who had fallen head over heels in love with a man she knew to be exciting and dangerous.

She should have listened to her instincts. Exciting, dangerous men did not normally make good husbands. But neither, she thought, striving to be fair, did excitable, passionate adolescents make reasonable wives.

For possibly the thousandth time she wondered why on earth he had married her. And for the thousandth time she slotted the question into the 'too-hard' category.

The taste of humiliation bitter in her mouth, she thought sickly that he needn't have been so blunt. 'Follow him barefoot through the world' had been right. He thought her just like her mother, and he despised her for it.

She was shivering as she got into a warm dressing-gown. Her eyes travelled unseeingly around the quiet room with its lace pillows and white roses, their palest pink hearts exuding a faint, sweet fragrance.

Giving in to anguish was not going to help. She was shocked—naturally, the sight of Caine after all these years had been enough to set her spinning. And his revelations about her uncle were reason enough to make her feel this icy lump compounded of fear and disillusion in the middle of her chest.

She moved away from the French chest of drawers that served as her dressing-table, and walked heavily over to the window, looking out across the lovely view of Auckland basking lazily in the autumn sun, the harbour blue as sapphires between the islands and the isthmus.

Next door someone was playing tennis; she could hear the thwock, thwock, thwock of the ball as it went from end to end of the court, and laughter, and the sounds of thudding feet. Never before had she looked out in indifference, but this time she was so lost in thought that she saw nothing beyond the white of her knuckles as she gripped the sill.

Now she had to try to work out what to do. The first thing to do was contact her uncle, somewhere in the Pacific Ocean off Samoa. Until she had spoken to him she had no way of knowing what his plans were—if he had any. But surely he must have some sort of contingency plan ready, some way of dealing with Caine? Caine was not the sort of man to write off a debt, especially not one owed by a man he despised.

Petra wiped the slow tears away. Shuddering, cold, she recalled Caine's expression as he spoke of her uncle; he was ruthlessly intent, not, she thought, so much on regaining the money as on making Laurence Stanhope suffer.

And taking Stanhope's from him would certainly make her uncle suffer. That would be bad enough, but Aunt Kath would be desolated.

Purposefully she paced across the room, and picked up the telephone receiver. Five minutes later she was speaking to her uncle, handicapped by the fear that someone might be able to overhear, terrified that she would say something that might increase his worries.

There was no tactful, gentle way to lead into the subject. After the greetings she said urgently, 'Uncle Laurence, Caine is back. And he says he wants the money.'

There was a moment's stark silence before he said sharply, the aggression failing to hide a thin note of fear, 'What? What money?'

All hope died in her breast. 'The money you borrowed from him. A million dollars, remember?'

She waited, hearing her pulse beat in her ears. He blustered, 'I don't know what you're talking about.'

'Uncle Laurence, please. I know about it.'

Another silence, then he said heavily, 'So you believe him rather than me.'

It hurt to say it, but she blinked back the tears and whispered, 'I'm afraid I do. What are you going to do about it?'

'Don't you worry about——'

'Uncle Laurence,' she cried, 'I *have* to worry about it. If I hadn't been married to Caine he wouldn't have lent you the money. So some of the responsibility is mine.'

'Don't be a fool,' he snapped. 'Fleming lent me the money because he thought it was all going to come to him one day—Stanhope's, everything.'

She bit her lip. 'Well, it sounds as though it still might,' she said quietly.

'If you'd stayed married to him, yes. But when you divorced him you dropped me right in it.'

She flinched at the accusing note in his voice, accepting with her heart as well as her brain the fact that he had done this thing.

'Don't worry about it,' he went on harshly. 'Leave him to me to deal with.'

Vague, inchoate suspicions floated through Petra's mind. She asked tonelessly, 'Can you pay him back the money?'

'That's my business.'

'Please, I need to know.'

Her uncle said curtly, 'I can't talk now, your aunt's almost in the room. Take no notice of Fleming, and don't worry.'

And he hung up. Petra sat for a long moment staring down at the receiver before replacing it. She walked slowly down the stairs to the tiny outdated kitchen. After making a pot of tea, she sat down limply. The headache she had lied about was real now, throbbing away behind one eye with the prospect of becoming much worse unless she took something for it.

Two strong painkillers later she drank her tea, her eyes fixed with dreamy, slightly dazed concentration on a blackbird digging vigorously amongst the sweet williams outside her window. A snowflake acacia was opening its white powder-puffs of flowers to the approaching dusk, sending forth a musky sweetness to attract the moths that fertilised them.

The noise of the traffic had died away. Petra was horrified to find herself weeping softly, hopelessly, drearily. She blew her nose, hating the tears that ached in her throat, blaming them on the headache and the shocks of the day. Self-pity was an emotion she despised, fighting it with every weapon at her disposal, but occasionally it sneaked up on her.

What were they going to do? Her uncle's bluster hadn't rung true; intuitively she knew that he had no money to pay off the loan. But she felt morally obliged to do what she could to pay it off. She looked around her shabby sitting-room wondering how much the house would bring. Not a lot, but she would have to put it on the market as soon as the weekend was over. And she would sign the trust money over to Caine, too. She was young and strong, she earned good money; she could pay him more back out of her salary.

It was not fair that he should lose out because her uncle had forced him to marry her.

So she washed up, checked the locks downstairs, and went up to bed, while all around thousands of people prepared for their Saturday night with eager anticipation.

Her last thought was whether her uncle had lied to Caine, too; *had* he told him that they had conspired together to lure Caine into marriage? But why? It seemed a thoroughly stupid thing to do, unless he thought that Caine would take such an insult tamely, weighing it against the social advantages of being married to a Stanhope.

He had mistaken his man, if that was so. Caine was far too proud. It was Uncle Laurence who considered birth and breeding to be important, not Caine. He had already proved that he was any man's equal.

At last Petra slept, waking an hour later to the ring of the telephone. But when she lifted the receiver no one spoke, although she could hear breathing. Fear kicked in her stomach; she managed to control it enough to stay as silent as the person at the other end, and hang up.

Almost immediately it rang again, and again, four times in all, but she refused to answer. It fell silent then, but it was almost morning before she managed to get back to sleep.

CHAPTER SIX

THE impatient summons of the telephone woke Petra. After a horror-stricken moment she managed to convince herself that even if it was the man who had breathed at her last night she was in no danger. Men like that were poor, sad creatures, unable to get their pleasure in the usual ways. But her mouth was dry and her hand shook as she picked up the receiver.

'Hello,' she said huskily.

'Petra, it's Tracey Porter here; I'm so sorry if I woke you up.'

Blazing relief. Settling back against the pillows, Petra listened as Tracey continued, 'We're having a barbecue this evening, just a little spontaneous affair, and we'd love you and David to come.'

'I don't think——' She didn't have to think, she knew she wasn't going, but before she could come up with an excuse Tracey interrupted.

'I realise you probably have something else on your plate, but this could be good for the Fund. Cathy Ferrers will be there, you know—she used to be Cathy Durrant. You do know her, don't you?'

'Yes. Vaguely.' They had attended the same school, but Cathy had always been one of the movers and shakers; Aunt Kath had referred to her as 'fast'. They had not been friends. Cathy was the grandchild of one of the old pirate merchants, and had been left his huge estate, much of which she had incorporated into a trust that dealt out a considerable amount of money to assorted charities.

Tracey continued smoothly, 'I thought it would be a wonderful opportunity to talk to her. Your idea of a foundation that helps couples with parenting skills could well appeal to her, especially as you've given such a lot of consideration as to how the media could be used. Her husband is a playwright. We've been trying to latch on to her for ages, as you know. Which is where you might come in handy. You do, after all, know her.'

Petra nodded, relinquishing with resignation the prospect of a quiet evening at home. 'Yes, all right, I'll come; but David is away for the weekend,' she said. 'What time?'

A little thread of disappointment dampened down the anticipation in Tracey's voice. 'Oh, about fourish, fiveish. Thank you, Petra. I hope you aren't giving up too exciting an evening for this.'

Petra made a non-committal murmur, and hung up, thinking that she disliked Tracey quite alarmingly. But she would go to her barbecue, because Cathy Ferrers just might be persuaded that the Fund could do with some of that money.

She spent the day working in her little garden, lovingly tending its manicured perfection, the cold foreboding in her heart eased a little by the delicate new blooms on her sasanqua camellia, their earthy scent as sweet and fresh as a florist's shop, and the discovery of the tiny pink and white blooms of the Neapolitan cyclamens at its feet. The telephone stayed silent, and slowly her sense of violation eased.

In the afternoon she played tennis with an old friend, then, with immense reluctance, got ready for the evening, grimacing as she pulled on a watermelon chiffon skirt and shirt, sliding her feet into sandals a deeper shade of the same colour, pinning her hair back from her face in a smoothly sophisticated style.

Her subtle mask of cosmetics was soon in place, albeit toned down to suit the comparative informality of the occasion. Normally she would have worn trousers and a silk shirt to a barbecue, but Tracey's idea of informality was drinking out of Scandinavian crystal instead of Waterford, so Petra dressed accordingly.

Sure enough, Tracey was in a sari that suited her dark, sultry good looks perfectly. Great golden hoops hung in her ears, and on her pretty feet she wore exotic golden sandals.

Beside her Petra felt positively restrained. Spontaneous, my foot! she thought vulgarly as her hostess ushered her through to an enormous terrace carefully landscaped to look like a jungle. This was no impromptu, unplanned occasion. Milling about were at least a hundred people, all elegantly dressed. So why had she and David been invited at the last minute?

She knew many of the crowd there, and set herself to be charming, smiling and chatting with an untouched drink in her hand, ignoring the essential loneliness of someone who was by herself when most of the others were in couples.

No sign of Cathy Ferrers. Petra was beginning to wonder whether the whole evening was going to be a waste of time when her eye was caught by the arrogant tilt of a dark head across the terrace. Her vision blurred, then cleared. Yes, it was Caine, and he was not alone. With him was a wonderful gypsyish creature about six feet tall with a wild mane of red hair above magnificent cheekbones and a lush, pouting mouth. The latest model sensation.

Like a spear of fire, jealousy stabbed through the mask of composure that was Petra's trademark straight into her heart. Her eyes narrowed; she had taken a step forwards before she realised what she was doing, and forcibly halted that impetuous, totally unforgivable approach. She dropped her eyes to the white fingers clasping her glass, noting with vague distaste the death-grip she had on the thing.

Trembling, racked by emotions she had never experienced before, Petra lifted the glass and drank the liquid straight down, gasping a little at its potency, but welcoming the quick bite of the alcohol, the sudden flush that swept the pallor from her skin.

But her eyes stayed fixed on Caine's dark face as he smiled down at the splendid, sultry face of the woman who laughed and swayed towards him as though she was incapable of doing anything else. Petra recognised his smile. There was indulgence in it, and a sexual potency that sent her pulse-rate soaring.

'Oh, God,' Petra heard herself say beneath her breath. 'Oh, you fool!'

Whatever love she had felt for him might have died beneath his brutal treatment of it, but the sexual attraction was still there, the unbidden, in-built recognition that this man could do to her what no other had managed to.

The model laughed again, shaking her glorious mane of hair, and, with a gesture that hinted of the intimacy between them, laid two slender fingers over the clear-cut, sensual line of his mouth.

Petra winced and turned away, unable to watch any longer. Her first impulse was to think up an excuse and go, but wiser counsel prevailed. She attached herself to a group of people she knew slightly, and managed to appear as if she was enjoying herself, although her nerves were strung so tightly that she thought they might snap.

At last, just as she wondered whether she might be able to slip away, she saw Cathy Ferrers arrive with her husband. At last, thank God!

So she was ready five minutes later when she heard Tracey's voice behind her.

'And of course I don't have to introduce Petra,' she was saying sweetly. 'Petra, dear——'

Turning, Petra pinned her social smile firmly to her face, wishing that she didn't feel rather sleazy about this 'unpremeditated' meeting.

But the couple with her hostess was not the Ferrers; instead, Caine was looking down at her, his expression dispassionate, no emotion visible in those clear, depthless eyes.

Petra's smile slipped a little, then firmed. 'Hello, Caine,' she said calmly. 'How are you?'

'Fine. And you?'

In spite of the charming smile he gave her she couldn't tell what he was thinking, but then she had never been able to. The cold, calculating brain behind the striking face was locked to bystanders.

'And this is Simone.' Tracey slid the introduction in like a knife-blade, watching with an avidity she couldn't conceal. 'Simone, this is Petra Stanhope.'

The petulant beauty looked bored, but flashed her wonderful smile as she murmured a response to Petra's pleasant greeting.

Caine's smile didn't warm his expression. The tall model flicked shrewd eyes from the still, impassive face of the woman in front of her to the greedy, barely controlled curiosity in Tracey's. Her brows lifted; she sent a pertly languishing look up to Caine, her lush, sultry mouth tucked in at the corners as she tried to hide her amusement.

Petra was horrified to realise that she felt like grabbing the girl and shaking her, then hurling her as far as her strength would send her.

The force of her reaction appalled her. She had got over Caine; she had divorced him, for heaven's sake! Oh, she would probably always be susceptible to his sort of bold masculine attraction, but that was a purely physical response, encoded in her genes. So why should she be so angry just because some woman made it more than obvious that she too was affected by his lean male potency?

'Caine and Gerald are having talks about boring old business things,' Tracey informed nobody in particular, her eyes darting eagerly from Petra's face to the enigmatic masculine one above, carved with bold strokes from teak. 'So naturally we asked him along to our little barbecue. It's so kind of you to come, Caine, when I know you have such a lot to fit into your trip back home. How long are you staying?'

His pale eyes narrowed a second. 'That depends entirely on Petra,' he said, watching her.

She had never had more reason to bless her shiny, impervious shield of composure. It took all her self-command to produce the small smile that curled her lips—aloof, yet with a hint of mockery in it.

'Nonsense,' she replied sweetly. 'Don't tease, Caine.' And stayed silent.

With alert interest Simone asked, 'You two know each other well?'

'Oh, Petra and I were married years ago,' he explained casually, never taking his eyes from Petra's composed face.

Simone ran expert eyes up and down Petra's erect figure. She commented cheerfully, 'Well, clearly you've always fancied clothes-horses.'

In spite of the jealousy that gnawed at her, Petra suspected that given different circumstances she might have liked the model.

Of course Caine should have been a trifle taken aback by the model's frankness, and, of course, he wasn't. 'Yes,' he agreed amiably. 'Although Petra wasn't quite so elegant when we were married. That band-box appearance is a new development.' And not one I like, his tone implied.

Petra gave a soft, unamused laugh. 'Youth can get away with the tousled look; it loses its appeal once you hit twenty-five.'

'You sound as though you're running downhill,' he said with cool deliberation. 'You're only twenty-six.'

He made a thorough survey of her before ranging a little further, his pale eyes fixing on to Tracey's fascinated face. It must have been difficult for her to stay silent, but no doubt she was terrified she might miss something if she even thought of carrying out any duties as a hostess, Petra thought savagely.

But, enthralled though Tracey was, she stepped back with involuntary nervousness when Caine caught her in that lethal tiger's smile. 'Thanks for the party, Mrs Porter,' he said negligently, his voice level and contemptuous. 'Simone and I are on our way.' His eyes pinned Petra down. 'Can I give you a lift?'

'No,' Petra said above the muffled litany of Tracey's objections. 'I brought my car.'

'OK, I'll see you into it.' He looked down at the model. 'Ready?'

After a quick glance at Petra, Simone transferred her gaze to Caine's autocratic face. Something like amusement glimmered in the tilted green eyes. 'Yes,' she said laconically, shrugging her magnificent shoulders.

Tracey said agitatedly, 'Cathy Ferrers——'

'I'll ring her,' Petra assured her, smiling, aware that her smile didn't reach her eyes, but with no idea of just how cold that made them. 'Goodnight, Tracey.'

Caine escorted them both out to the pavement, put Petra into her car, said a brusque 'Goodnight', then watched her drive off before striding along with Simone to his vehicle.

Finding them for a second in her rear-vision mirror, Petra admitted savagely that the model was much better-suited physically to Caine than she had been. In some ways, she thought, narrowly missing a car as she suffered a flashback to maddened nights spent in his arms. Was the luscious Simone going to find out that Caine had all the endurance and subtlety of a hunter, the padding, prowling sensuality of the panther, combined with an explosive passion that sent a woman to ecstasy and beyond?

Perhaps, she thought with curled lip, he would display some of that 'innovation' that had so enthralled Jan Pollard—now Jan Brewster—who apparently still hankered after his particular brand of sexuality. Join the club, Petra thought sourly.

But that way lay madness. She was not going to muddle her mind with memories.

And she was not going to show Tracey how furious she was with her, either, even though her nasty little plot had worked. No doubt Tracey was even now regaling a select group of cohorts with the tale of the exciting little incident.

Although Caine's blunt departure—and the unspoken narrow-eyed threat that had preceded it—might just make her hold her tongue. He was not the sort of man you tangled with, not if you wanted to keep your hide unscarred.

Before she went to bed she set the answerphone, just in case the intruder tried again. And, sure enough, fifteen minutes after she had turned the light off, the wretched thing rang again. Her heart gave a great lurch. Biting her lip, she stayed still, not moving until the summons died away. She tried to convince herself that it was a friend who didn't want to leave a message, but an unpleasant supposition crawled into her mind and wouldn't go away. Could the man who harrassed her see her window? Did he know when she went to bed? In spite of the sturdy common sense that told her she was in no danger it took her some hours to get off to sleep. There were no further rings.

Although there were no more phone calls, the next two nights were a tiring saga of restless sleep and violent, too easily recalled dreams. Thoroughly glad that the Easter break was over, Petra rang a land agent and made an appointment to see her after work that evening, then called the lawyer who looked after the small trust her father had left for her and asked him a few pertinent questions.

'Yes,' he said when she'd finished, 'you're right, you can dissolve your trust—it's easy enough to do under New Zealand law as you're the only beneficiary. But why do you want to?'

'I need the money,' she told him in a cool voice.

He hesitated. 'You could borrow against the trust.'

'No.'

'Are you sure? You'd better come in——'

'No,' she cut him off incisively. 'I've made up my mind.'

He tried to persuade her otherwise, but her inflexible tone finally convinced him that she knew what she was doing. 'All right,' he said with resignation. 'It will take a little time.'

'How long?'

'Give me a month or so, as there's no one else concerned.'

She had to be content with that. Once she had hung up she pencilled a few figures down, then pulled out her diary for the coming week. There were several business meetings, and on Saturday the Fund was holding its Fancy Dress Ball at the museum; she had to spend most of the day decorating the huge marble halls that the museum was allowing them to use. David would be back by then; she sighed, thinking that it would make her life a lot easier if she and David Carey could only fall in love with each other instead of remaining obstinately platonic friends.

But now, in his mid-thirties, he was not ever likely to marry. Years ago he had confided that the only reason he would consider giving up his bachelor existence would be to father children, and admitted that as time passed he found even that an insufficient reason for losing his independence.

'It's just that,' he had said, 'the women I love, like you, I don't seem to want, and the women I want I certainly don't love.'

'You want to have your cake and eat it,' she had accused, smiling.

He shrugged gracefully. 'I'm afraid it's true.'

Amusing and witty, he knew when to be silent. They frequently went out together, gaining from some people the reputation of being lovers. Petra didn't care. She liked him immensely, and their relationship suited them both.

He also knew his way around the financial labyrinth better than most. When he rang her late in the afternoon she waited until all the preliminaries were over before asking, 'David, how is Stanhope's doing?'

His silence told her more than she wanted to know.

'Why do you ask?' he said finally, in the cautious tone she associated with answers no one wanted to give.

'I need to know,' she said thinly.

He sighed. 'Not too well, I'm afraid. Your uncle is getting old. And to be brutally frank he has never been the man his father was. He's a good, traditional businessman, and for years that was enough, but it's not now. He should have gone under about eight years ago, but the business took on a new lease of life.'

She bit her lip so hard that the blood tasted salt in her mouth. 'And now?'

'To survive Stanhope's needs to be shaken up from the top to the bottom; it needs new designers, new executives, and a new managing director.'

'I see,' she said dully. 'Thanks.'

She heard the shrug in his voice. 'I don't know why he doesn't put you in charge. He certainly couldn't do any worse.'

She gave a ghost of a laugh. 'Oh, thank you for the faint praise! I doubt if I could do it—my expertise isn't in that field. Anyway, it's academic—Uncle Laurence just doesn't believe that women are any good at business. Thanks, anyway.'

'Come out to dinner with me tonight.'

She hesitated in her turn, then said, 'I don't think I'm going to be very good company.'

'Now, since when have we worried about that?' he chided. 'I'll pick you up at seven. Wear something pretty.'

Later, the land agent looked around her small domain with a brisk, impersonal eye, before saying crisply, 'I think the best thing you can try for here is a developer. The situation is superb, but the house is certainly not worthy of it. Now that property is starting to boom again you should get quite a good price for it.' She named a sum of money that made Petra wince. The amount left after she had paid her mortgage was nowhere near enough to repay Caine, even with the money from her trust fund.

Misunderstanding her, the agent said briskly, 'Look, the kind of person who buys in Remuera is not going to want to live in a cottage, charming though it is.'

'I know,' Petra said wearily. 'It's all right. Advertise it.'

After she had filled in the forms and seen the agent off the property she walked around the garden, fighting the tears that welled up in her eyes. This was no time to give in to her emotions; she had to stay controlled, because some way or another she was going to have to pay Caine off.

The last thing she wanted to do was dress up and go out, but she couldn't bear the thought of staying at home while her safe, stable life crumbled around her.

And David, she thought with gratitude, was safety personified.

When he arrived he looked her over, a faint smile on his handsome face, before kissing her cheek. 'All flags flying, Petra?' he said. 'Good for you.'

So he knew Caine was back. She smiled, but said nothing, knowing that he wouldn't bring the matter up unless she did. They respected each other's privacy.

'Yes,' she replied simply.

They ate at a very expensive, very private restaurant. David told her of his trip to Sydney, she told him of her experience at the races, mentioning Caine's name with an indifference that was hard won. She drank a little wine, and pushed her food around her plate.

'Care to talk?' he asked gently.

Her mouth trembled, but she forced it to smile. 'I don't know that there's anything to talk about,' she said with a try at her usual crispness. 'Unless you can find a way for me to acquire a large amount of money very quickly.'

'How much?'

She told him, and he whistled softly. 'No,' he said quietly. 'Things are looking up, but money's still tight. And unless you have security——'

She shook her head. 'No. Oh, who am I kidding? There's no way I could pay even the interest on a loan like that, let alone any principal.'

'I gather this has something to do with the sudden arrival of Caine Fleming on the scene?' He noted her sudden stiffness. 'And possibly with the fact that Stanhope Ltd had an unexpected easing of its financial problems eight years ago?'

Petra looked up into his shrewd eyes. 'Yes,' she said beneath her breath.

'Damn! I wish I could help——'

'Oh, David.' Her eyes filled with tears as she reached a hand out to cover his. Smiling ironically, he enclosed hers between his two warm ones. 'I do love you,' she murmured.

There was a subdued bustle somewhere in the big room, and she looked up to meet Caine's eyes drilling into her with the force of an antarctic storm as the head-waiter showed him and his red-headed mistress to a table. The breath stopped in Petra's throat. Caine's eyes flicked from her pale face to her and David's linked hands.

He was making her nervous. He was ruining her tranquillity. He was making her remember things she would far rather forget. And he watched her with eyes like shards of ice—cold, penetrating, stabbing through the shiny mask of worldliness she had cultivated over the years, trying to probe into the shrinking soul beneath.

Lifting her head proudly, she met the dark threat in his expression with a cold, still hauteur that should have stopped him in his tracks. Instead he said something to the model, and veered off to where Petra sat with David, hands still clasped. She resisted the almost irresistible compulsion to jerk her hand away from David's.

'Who is it?' David asked quickly, but before she could answer Caine said in a smooth, deadly voice, 'Good evening, Petra.'

'Hello, Caine.' Furious because her voice wobbled, she couldn't produce a smile.

He stopped by the table and looked down at them, using his height and his crackling social persona to intimidate. 'And who is your friend?' he asked urbanely.

'This is David Carey,' she said, hating the defensive note in her voice, but unable to hide it. 'David, have you met Caine Fleming?'

Without undue haste David relinquished her hand, and stood. Not as tall as Caine, he possessed little of his autocratic charisma, but he was not intimidated. The two men shook hands, both surveying the other with an unsmiling stare.

'I want to see you,' Caine stated, turning abruptly to Petra.

She raised her brows. 'Very well. When?'

'As soon as possible.' He was observing her narrowly, the gleaming silver eyes hooded, but his stance, something about the way he looked at David and then at her reminded her of a bird of prey, circling slowly and effortlessly before the screaming strike that killed its defenceless target.

'Ring me,' she told him quietly, unable to work out exactly what was going on, but refusing absolutely to make an appointment with one man when she was with another.

'I'll do that,' he said, showing his teeth. He gave a curt nod to David, said, 'Carey,' and left them, striding noiselessly across the room, a predator in the midst of a herd of deer.

'Phew!' David exclaimed, sitting down, his perceptive gaze never leaving her face.

'I'm sorry,' she muttered helplessly. 'I don't know why he came across.' Her eyes drifted across to the model Simone, who was laughing at Caine, apparently not at all upset at being left.

'I do,' David said, smiling at some private joke. 'He's heard the gossip, and he wanted to check me out.'

'No, not Caine.'

He grinned. 'Why not?'

Petra gestured a little, unable to find the words. 'There's no need—I mean, he doesn't——'

'He strikes me as being a very possessive man.'

'He has nothing,' she said with a bite in her tone, 'to be possessive about. We are divorced.'

'Who did the divorcing?'

Her shoulders moved uneasily. 'I did, but he——' She stopped, her mouth tightening into a hard line. 'He was the one who ended our marriage,' she finished.

David was watching her with a sympathy that she found irritating, almost intrusive. 'For a good reason?'

She had carefully not considered this aspect, hiding from it, and the fact that it was David who was forcing her to face it made her feel as though he was betraying her. 'He—thought so,' she said at last with a vast unwillingness.

Had it been a good reason? Oh, she could understand his sense of betrayal when he thought she had deliberately seduced him into marriage so that her uncle could borrow from him. But if he had really loved her he would have listened to her.

But he had not let her say anything. He had called her a whore and thrown her out.

So he had not really loved her. He had used the loan to hide his real reason for ending their marriage—the fact that he found her passion for him degrading and disgusting.

For some reason the pain that this engendered still hurt as much as it had when she first accepted it. Caine had wanted her, and he had married her because her uncle, for reasons of his own, had insisted that that was what an honourable man would do. And because in his own way Caine was honourable, too. But his desire had been sated, and in a remarkably short time the revulsion she could remember from her mother's lovers had driven him to leave her.

'And do *you* think that he had good reason?' David probed.

Eyes averted, she sipped some wine, the cool liquid running easily down her dry throat. 'No,' she said quietly. 'We were too young—I was too young, but if he had loved me he would have given me another chance. He would at least have listened to me.'

David said just as quietly, 'Sometimes a person loves too much to forgive.'

'That's not love,' she countered acidly. 'That's possessiveness. Let's not talk about it any more, David.'

'Very well, but I think perhaps Fleming has every intention of discussing things; I thought it might help clarify things if you talked it over.'

She smiled with difficulty. 'Oh, he won't get personal, it's merely business.'

They left soon after. As she walked out Petra gave Caine and his companion a bland smile, suffering the scalding intensity of his regard until she went out into the cool night air.

The wretched fear that assailed her every night now made her persuade David into coming inside for coffee. A quick glance at the answerphone showed no red light, and she caught back a sigh of relief as it threatened to break free.

From behind her he asked, 'Do you mind if I turn on the television set? There's an interview I want to see, and my video has died on me.'

'Feel free.'

But when she brought the tray into the sitting-room it was to see the unyielding angles and planes of Caine's face, and hear the crisp, cutting logic of his argument as he demolished the interviewer.

'They must have pre-recorded it,' David said, switching the set off.

She nodded. 'Do you want to watch?'

'No. I think I've seen enough of your ex-husband for the night. Ah, that looks good.'

The coffee was delicious, but they drank it in silence, Petra unable to rid her mind of the way Caine had smiled at Simone, and the crackling aggression of his approach to David.

She had just set her cup down when the telephone rang. Her stomach lurched. For a moment she stared at it, then reluctantly, her hand revealing a fine tremor, she picked up the receiver. 'Hello?'

There was no reply, although she could hear the breathing on the other end. The blood drained from her face as she fixed her eyes on David. 'Who is there?' she asked curtly.

'What is it?' David asked, the words coming hard and fast.

There was a sharp intake of breath from the unknown person at the other end, and then the sound of the receiver being slammed home.

Petra's hand trembled as she put the receiver down. 'Just a heavy-breather,' she said, trying to sound cool and sophisticated. 'He hung up when he heard you.'

David swore under his breath. 'Is this the first time?'

She told him, and he asked, 'Have you contacted Telecom?'

'No,' she said. 'He hasn't rung for a couple of nights, and I thought he'd stopped.'

The *brr* of the telephone made her jump and press a hand to her heart, her pulses going haywire.

'Don't answer,' David commanded sharply. 'And come home with me. Tomorrow you can contact Telecom and get them to do something about it, but there's no need for you to stay in the house and be intimidated by a creep like this.'

The ringing went on and on and on. White-faced, nausea grabbing at her stomach, Petra stared at the telephone.

David cursed, then, when it was obvious the caller wasn't going to give up, caught up the receiver and barked, 'She's not going to answer.' Slamming it down, he jerked it off the hook before the caller could dial again. 'Come on,' he ordered firmly. 'Get your toothbrush and something to wear tomorrow, and we'll head for home.'

Petra was so shaken that she obeyed him, and, still shivering, allowed herself to be driven the ten minutes to his flat, thankful for the warmth of his arm about her as he walked beside her up the footpath. She was so affected by the incident that the sound of a car engine starting up, followed immediately by the piercing squeal of abused tyres brought a choked little gasp to her lips. Instinctively she shrank into David's side.

'It's all right,' he said soothingly, dropping a kiss on to her forehead as he unlocked the door. 'It's just some young hoon showing off.'

The hair on the back of her neck prickled; swallowing, she told herself firmly not to be an idiot. But when she lay in David's comfortable spare room she thought bitterly that her sanctuary had been well and truly desecrated. Not that it mattered much, because soon it wouldn't be hers any longer. A sob caught in her throat. Turning her face into the pillow, she wept as though her heart would break.

After a while she drifted off into a hag-ridden, restless sleep, waking too often and too quickly to lie with a dry mouth and thumping heart listening to the sounds of the wind in the eaves as she tried to clear her brain of leftover snatches of nightmare.

Of course it wasn't so bad the next morning, although daylight was ushered in with a downpour of rain that didn't ease until she was in David's car on the way back to her house, and then only to reveal a sky sullen with the promise of more.

She told herself that she wasn't going to, but as soon as she was inside her gaze flew to the telephone. It stayed silent, but the little red light from the answerphone flicked on and off, on and off.

'I set it last night while you were getting your toothbrush.' David answered her unspoken query. 'I'll check it. You go on upstairs; there's no need for you to listen.'

His protectiveness was sweet, but Petra was no longer a child. 'No, I'll listen,' she said, going over and pressing the button.

Five times the unknown caller had tried to contact her. Petra bit her lip, fighting back a wave of sick panic.

'Ring Telecom right now,' David insisted, frustration and contempt plain in his voice.

Petra shook her head. 'I'll be late for work. I'll do it at work, I promise.'

'I suppose so.' But he hovered, clearly uneasy, then asked suddenly, 'Why don't you spend the next week or so with me?'

It was the easy way out, the appeal to the protective male, the eager surrender to his strength, and Petra was tempted, but the land agent would be bringing people through, and anyway she was damned if she was going to be driven from her home by a man who was so ineffectual that he had to get his kicks from terrorising women over the telephone.

She smiled mistily at this man whom she loved like a brother, and insisted, 'I'll be all right, I promise.'

David didn't like it, but eventually he left, taking with him her promise to contact him if the caller rang again.

It was horrible to feel so threatened within her own house, but stoically Petra forced her lingering fear down, even managing to get to work on time. At least, she thought hollowly, she hadn't had time to worry about the reason Caine wanted to see her again!

But at mid-morning, when he contacted her, she was so nervous that she found it difficult to speak. It was impossible to learn anything from his voice, which was aloof and uncommunicative, and because she wanted to get it over and done with she agreed to meet him for lunch that day. By the time one o'clock arrived her normal serenity had become a grim determination to control her emotions.

He was waiting inside the restaurant, dressed in the impersonal smartness of a business suit, but he stood out among all the other suited men about him with an easy, unstudied authority that was partly based on his splendid physical presence, but rooted much more securely in the strength of his character, the dark intensity that was a primal force at the centre of his personality.

So many facets, Petra thought as he stood to allow her to follow the headwaiter in. He was so difficult to understand, this tall man with dark hair that blazed in the sun, with icy colourless eyes and that surprisingly sensuous mouth set in features as tough and lethal as an axe-blade...

And with the soul of a puritan, unyielding, refusing to compromise. Sensuality and austerity—a tormenting paradox in his character.

No wonder she had failed so miserably as his wife.

But then, apart from the fact that he was a magnificent lover, his instinctive knowledge honed by experience to expertise, he hadn't been such a good husband, either, and his final folly had been his conviction that she had married him for money when she had been so besotted that she would have married him without a job, without a penny to his name!

Holding her mouth firmly under control, she sat down, letting her eyes drift around the room. This was power-eating, she thought; men in suits, women in the equivalent, silent, unobtrusive waiters, food eaten without appreciation while the diners talked business. And Caine was very much at home.

'You look tired,' he observed, watching her with shadowed eyes.

She shrugged as the waiter brought menus and gave his little spiel about the blackboard-specials. When he had gone she opened the menu to stare unseeingly down at the page.

'Did Carey keep you up late?' he asked, a note of disturbing intensity in his voice.

'No,' she answered calmly, and closed the menu. 'I'll have the fish and some salad, please.'

He looked across the room, and a waiter came scurrying up. 'Steak and fish and salads,' he ordered indifferently.

'Would you like some wine, madam, sir?' the wine-waiter asked, coming to a stop beside their table.

Caine looked at Petra. She shook her head, and he ordered mineral water for her and a beer for himself. When the water came she drank it eagerly, grateful for its cool easing of the dryness in her throat.

'Are you and Carey lovers?' he asked abruptly.

Petra's glance flew up to meet his, sank at the implacable glitter she saw there. 'That's none of your business,' she said huskily.

He shrugged. 'As it happens, it is.'

'Why?' She could barely get the word out as her throat had almost closed with tension.

He leaned back in the seat, watching her with the chilling impersonality of a statue, the only moving thing about him the glitter beneath his lashes. 'Because,' he said indifferently, 'I know how you can pay for your uncle's debt.'

An icy breath stole over her. 'And how is that?' she asked.

'You can marry me again.'

CHAPTER SEVEN

THE colour drained from Petra's face, taking all warmth with it. She stared at him, her eyes as huge and dark as a storm-tossed sea, searching the harshly hewn angles of his face for some sign that this was an awful, humiliating joke.

But he met her eyes with a cold purposefulness, and she saw that he meant it. For a moment hope, like an incandescent flash of lightning, surged through her, but she had been betrayed by hope too many times in the past, and she refused to follow it down that particular pathway again.

'What about Simone?' she blurted.

His eyes narrowed, but he said calmly, 'What about her?'

'How is she going to feel about this—proposal?'

'Are you asking whether she's my mistress? She's not. We met in San Francisco a couple of months ago, and liked each other. I looked her up when I came back, and we've been out together a couple of times. That's as far as it goes. But even if she had been my mistress it is no business of yours. I have no intention of being unfaithful.'

His voice was level and unemotional, but she flushed. Starkly she said, 'I don't want to marry you again.'

'Ah, but this time there will be no hidden agenda,' he said coolly. 'I'll know exactly why you've married me— to get your uncle off the hook. I won't expect anything more from you than you can give, so there'll be no disillusion——'

'Caine,' she interrupted, trembling, 'don't.'

'Don't what?'

'Don't—be so cruel. I can't marry you. I've put my house on the market and I'm liquidating my trust fund. It won't be——'

'What the hell are you talking about?' His voice was molten, as explosive as the white-hot heat of his glare.

Petra bit her lip, but said valiantly, 'With what Uncle Laurence can get for his house and——'

'His house is heavily mortgaged,' he interrupted, savagely *sotto voce*.

She lifted her eyes to him, her face unconsciously pleading, saying, 'It's all I can manage. I know it's not enough, but——'

The waiter arriving with their food realised, as all good waiters did, that this was no place for him, and disappeared with an alacrity that would have amused her any other time. But Petra was too strung-up to appreciate it; she was watching Caine's expression, noting with wary fascination how that deadly fury had been brought under restraint so swiftly, all traces leaving his lean, clever face as though it had never existed.

She understood now how he had become so powerful; this frightening control allied to brilliance and the kind of street-smart intuition he possessed must have made his climb almost easy for him.

'I suppose I should have realised that you'd bankrupt yourself to help them,' he said harshly.

Petra stared down at the food on her plate, unable to speak.

'However,' he continued, watching her closely, 'if marriage is too distasteful we could make another bargain.' His mouth tilted in a cool, ironic smile which didn't reach his eyes. 'You can pay off that debt by sleeping with me for as long as I like, and when I get tired of you we'll call it a day.'

Colour rolled up through her fine skin, then ebbed like an ice tide, taking with it the confidence and self-esteem she had built with such difficulty over the past eight years.

If she had ever wondered—and yes, why not admit it? she had spent quite a lot of the last years wondering what he thought of her—well, she had no need to wonder any longer. He thought her the whore he had called her when he'd left her, the woman who found it 'convenient' to love him, convenient to marry for money.

Fighting a desolation so intense that it had to show in her expression, she said through white lips, 'It's certainly not the most flattering proposition I've ever had. And the answer is no.'

'You want hearts and flowers?' He looked amused, nothing more, the lean face etched in lines of ironic appreciation. 'Sorry, princess, you've already had those. And don't try to tell me that you don't want me, because you do. You're as aware of me as I am of you, and you know how much that is.'

He watched with merciless eyes as she turned her head away, refusing to admit even to herself that he was right.

Quite calmly he finished, 'Whatever we had eight years ago is still there. It's time to get rid of it. Abstinence doesn't appear to be able to do the trick, so we'll try satiation.'

Anger, hot and rich and satisfying, broke through the mask of her composure. She said quietly, 'You bloody swine, Caine. I am not your whore to lie down with you because you want to scratch an itch. If you want that money so much——'

She stopped, because although he hadn't said anything the look on his face was enough to make the words freeze on her lips.

'The decision,' he said almost indifferently, 'is yours, princess. You have three choices: we marry, you become my mistress for as long as it takes you to earn the money your uncle owes me, or Laurence Stanhope goes messily bankrupt.'

The sheer, naked effrontery of his threat brought Petra's head up, her eyes snapping with a quick blaze of green, but he was eating his steak, apparently not at all impressed by her reaction. Then he looked up, and she saw no warmth, no softening in the glittering crystal of his gaze, nothing that gave her any comfort. He was without mercy.

'But Stanhope's has been his life——'

'Then he should have taken better care of it,' Caine cut in brutally. 'It's been going downhill ever since he inherited it from his father. He's used it as a milch cow to provide the money to keep him and your aunt in the expensive style they think the world owes them. He's always been incompetent, but now he's grown lazy as well, and Stanhope's is as close to bankruptcy as a firm can be and still keep going.'

Obviously it was no use appealing to his mercy. He had none. Petra pushed a piece of avocado around her plate, and said painfully, 'I have to think it over.'

'No. I want the answer now.' His voice was indifferent, but, for all that no emotion was visible in the lean, hard lines of his face, she knew he was feeling something—something so strong that the only way to control it was to refuse to admit that it existed.

Was it hatred? Or was it some other emotion, something like the feelings she had for him, feelings she didn't understand? Because he had left her so abruptly that her emotions had been frozen in limbo; she had not been able to accept them or change them, so when it came to Caine she was still the adolescent who had fallen head over heels in love and been cruelly, brutally rejected. And he was right, it was time to get rid of them. Perhaps his way, crude though it sounded, would at last lead to peace, of a sort.

Petra had never considered herself a gambler. Especially not when it came to emotions; she had her mother's experiences as a horrid warning that impetuosity was dangerous. But she said now, almost without volition, 'Very well, then; I'll marry you again.'

Something moved in the depths of his eyes, but his face remained immobile. 'Right,' he said calmly. 'I'll take you home to get your birth certificate; we'll need that for the marriage certificate. Arrange to have next week off, and we'll get married on Saturday.'

Appalled, she stared at him. 'It's too soon——'

'No,' he interrupted quietly, stopping the words on her lips. 'It's probably too late, but there's nothing we can do about that now.'

She bit her lip, wondering what he meant, yet unable to ask. The note of tired resignation in his voice struck a chord deep in her heart. It almost gave her hope.

Giving up on her meal, she drank the rest of the mineral water, using it to cover her nervousness. 'I don't know whether I'll be able to get next week off.'

His mouth quirked. If there had been any vulnerability in his voice a moment ago it was gone now. 'If you tell them it's important I'm sure you won't have any difficulty,' he drawled. 'Tell them you'll be on your honeymoon.'

Automatically she shook her head, and his smile hardened, became cynical. 'Perhaps not,' he agreed. 'Have you finished?'

'Yes.'

Summoned by another imperious look, the waiter came across, and within a couple of minutes they were outside. Rain spattered down on to the road. It fitted, Petra thought wearily, beginning to appreciate some of the more frightening implications of committing herself to marry Caine again.

'I'll drop you off,' he said, leading her to the BMW and opening the door for her.

But she knew that she couldn't go on with it. Something was wrong, something was making her so uneasy that she could barely sit beside him, all sorts of hideous fears gibbering at her from behind the half-closed doors of her mind. Lacing her hands painfully together in her lap, she said, 'Caine, I don't think marriage is a good idea. I—if you want me, I'll become your mistress.'

'It's too late to renege on the deal,' he replied calmly. 'I've changed my mind. I don't want you as a mistress.'

She turned her eyes from the windscreen to his implacable profile. 'Why?'

The corner of his mouth quirked in a movement as humourless as it was involuntary. 'Because I'd rather have you as a wife,' he said reasonably. 'So you have only two choices now. Leave your uncle to his just deserts, or marry me.'

She bit her lip, dragging her eyes back to the rainy streetscape outside. 'Then I have no choice,' she said, her voice trembling slightly. 'I'll marry you.'

'Yes, I knew you would.'

They were married at ten o'clock on Saturday morning in the register office. Petra wore her periwinkle blue suit, and Caine was elegant and sophisticated in a charcoal business suit. With them were Petra's oldest friend and her husband, winkled up from a sheep station near Raglan. None of Caine's relatives attended, not even the Andersons who had given him his first chance in life.

Afterwards they had lunch in a private room in a restaurant, a meal that was only rescued from disaster by Caine's urbanity, Petra's stern sense of duty, and the enthusiastic good cheer of the Simpsons.

'I like him,' Belinda muttered as she gave Petra a hug goodbye. To Caine she gave a kiss and a stern admonition, 'Take great care of her; she looks a bit fragile to me.'

'I'll look after her very well,' he promised, smiling at his wife as if she was the one good thing in his life.

Although the obscene caller had not tried to contact her since the night she spent at David's, nervousness and the strain of Caine's ultimatum had prevented Petra from sleeping much during the past few nights. So the night before she had taken a sleeping pill. She thought its effects must still be with her, because she was floating a little, feeling an odd sense of dislocation and distance. She rather liked it. The preceding days had been made unbearable by her convictions that she was embarking on the most horrific gamble in her life—one which she would pay for with pain and misery.

They said goodbye to the Simpsons out on the street, then Caine drove Petra back to her house. An hour before the wedding he had checked out of the luxury hotel where he had been staying, and brought a suitcase round. As the BMW turned up the drive she wondered whether he would expect to take her to bed right then, or whether he was going to wait until they had reached whatever destination he had chosen for their honeymoon. He had not touched her since that insulting proposal, had made no attempt to kiss her. Petra told herself that she was glad; she did not want to make love with him.

She knew nothing about their honeymoon except that he had told her, 'Take only casual clothes. Jeans, gumboots, that sort of thing.'

'Will I be expected to milk cows or chop wood?' she asked a little huskily, because the thought was not without charm.

He smiled aloofly. 'No, I'll do any wood-chopping that's necessary.'

So she had packed a suitcase with warm casual clothes, suitable for country pursuits.

'I'll get changed in your spare room,' he told her once they were inside the house.

Petra nodded, reprieved and grateful for it, she told herself sturdily as she walked up the stairs. In her room she changed into a pair of blue-green twill jodhpurs worn with a shirt a paler shade of the same colour, pulled on a turquoise waistcoat, and after a moment's thought took out a tweed jacket in the same blues and greens, finishing off with a pair of boots and a wide gold-buckled belt. It was a little outlandish, but she liked the outfit, and it gave her some much-needed confidence in herself.

When she came down he was standing in the kitchen drinking coffee, dominating the room. She recognised a kind of leashed impatience in him, a darkly masculine need for action that found some echo in the wilder regions of her heart.

In a light blue shirt and darker trousers, his only concession to the cool day a camel-coloured shearling coat, Caine looked rugged and dangerous, the clear grey of his eyes darkened to granite by the shadow of his lashes.

He also looked tired, the angular contours of his face hewn into deep relief. If Petra hadn't known that he never abused alcohol she might have believed him to be suffering from a hangover. Her heart did a funny, frightened flip in her breast, then settled down to beat double-time.

Although he gave her a comprehensive survey and his mouth quirked a little, he said nothing except, 'I've made you some coffee. Drink it up.'

'Yes.' But she hesitated, all her unease suddenly loud in her head.

'We've got a four-hour drive ahead of us,' he told her with another of those narrowed, intent stares. 'It'll be dark by the time we get there as it is.'

Nodding, she picked up the mug and drank. The coffee was a little strong, but it was refreshing, and she drained it, trying to convince herself that she had done the right thing.

The big BMW ate up the miles as he steered north across the harbour bridge. Petra burrowed back into the comfortable seat, looking out over the grey waters of the harbour and the leafy suburbia that bordered it. Caine had always liked to drive, bringing to it the physical authority that was so integral a part of him. Her eyes slid across to his lean hands, confident and skilful on the wheel, his attitude relaxed yet alert. If anything happened those finely sharpened reflexes would take over. She had total confidence in him.

Before long she began to feel sleepy. Several times she caught herself up with a guilty jerk as she nodded off, but at last the hum of the wheels on the road and the smoothly competent driving lulled her into unconsciousness.

The man beside her flicked a look at her profile. A grim smile carved itself into his cheeks. He put his foot down, and the powerful car leapt ahead.

Petra had no idea how long she slept, only that when she woke, stiff-necked and disoriented, all she could see through the thick dusk was the dark rise of hills alongside the road.

In fact, she took some time to realise where she was. She had been dreaming of a brooding menace, a saga of fear and flight, and she thought for some time that this was merely an extension of it. From beneath heavy eyelids she noted with a dull lack of interest the flash of the headlights against trees and banks, a metal road dotted with the shiny blackness of potholes filled with water. No lights shone comfortingly through the darkness, so wherever they were was well off the main roads.

An animal ran across the road. Swearing softly, Caine avoided it, and the jerk lifted her lashes. Etched against the faint light from the dashboard she could see the arrogant slash of his profile. Something—fear or attraction, she didn't know which—moved in the pit of her stomach.

She asked huskily, 'Where are we?'

'North of the Hokianga harbour.'

'Really in the backblocks.' Her voice was so brittle that it sounded as though it might break into shards. A gnawing nervousness struggled to emerge through the haze of sleep.

'About as far as you can go in Northland,' he agreed calmly.

'Where are we headed?'

'Past Herekino. I have a bach there on a run-down block of land.'

Her brain grappled sluggishly with the information. Through clumsy lips she asked, 'How far do we have to go?'

'A few more miles.'

Keep calm, she adjured herself. Keep calm and controlled, otherwise he'll trample all over you.

So she turned her head away, and watched the shades of night flash by. Soon she was drifting in a sort of stupor, half asleep, half waking, and the darkened countryside outside meant nothing any longer.

When she awoke she was lying on a wide double bed listening to the rain on a corrugated iron roof, the grey seepage of morning light almost painful to her eyes.

She was warm—the duvet pulled up to her chin saw to that—and she was clad, she discovered with a quick movement of her hand, in bra and pants.

Something else she discovered with that movement, too. She was not alone in the bed, and the man she had slept with appeared to have no clothes on at all.

Petra lay very still, oddly warmed by the human warmth of waking up next to him. But before long the first faint tendrils of fear wound their way through the lazy contentment. Why had Caine insisted on marriage, when he could have had what he wanted without it?

Perhaps because marriage gave him a sort of hold over her? She fought the fear down, willing herself to breathe slowly and evenly, concentrating on holding the fear at bay.

Caine was not an animal; she was not physically afraid of him. During their first marriage her transparent emotions had given him the upper hand. But that was a long time ago. Now, if she showed him that no matter what he did she would stay fully in control of her emotions and her life, then he would be forced to realise that she had changed, that she was no longer defenceless against his merciless charisma.

And perhaps it would redeem her a little, so that when he thought of her it was no longer as a lust-driven adolescent but as a responsible woman.

'I know you're awake,' he remarked conversationally.

Her heart fluttered, but she fought for control, releasing the yawn she had been holding in. In a voice husky with sleep she said, 'What time is it?'

'Morning,' he said laconically.

Because she couldn't think of anything else to do she yawned again. But the unspoken questions, the ones she couldn't ask, hovered on her tongue. What do you want? Are we going to make love?

'There should be enough hot water for you to shower if you want to.' There was a sardonic note in his voice that splintered along her nerve-ends.

Keep cool, she adjured her panicking inner self. Don't give him any indication that you are uneasy. He knows how to home in on weakness.

Pulling herself up on one elbow, she clutched the duvet protectively to her throat. Against the plain white pillowcase he looked a ruffian, piratical, his beard shadowing the uncompromising angles of his face, his eyes narrowed in an unsettling stare as he returned her guarded scrutiny with interest.

'Not afraid, Petra?' he asked, his smile a taunt.

She lifted an eyebrow. 'Why should I be afraid?'

'Does anything frighten you, my very composed wife? Can anything break through that shiny shell of self-sufficiency to the real woman beneath?'

'This *is* the real woman.' She hoped her fiercely beating heart wasn't apparent. 'What you see is what——' Warned by the cynical amusement in his eyes, she substituted a lame, 'what I am', for the words she had been going to use. What you see is what you get? Never.

'I don't believe you.'

She shrugged as best she could with the duvet clasped in a grip of iron. 'I don't know what you want,' she said, trying to infuse her tone with sweet reason.

His eyes blazed, hot diamonds in the lean angularity of his face. 'Perhaps I want to see something of the girl I married, who came fully, vibrantly alive in my arms, so passionate that she sold herself for a million dollars to quench the fires burning inside her.'

His words made her blood run cold, but, with the ease of practice and constant self-discipline, she parried, 'She doesn't exist any longer, Caine.'

'Are you saying I killed her?'

Her mouth parted, losing a little of its rigid restraint. His gaze sharpened, and Petra hastily composed her features. Something like disdain darkened the cool aquamarine of her eyes. 'No. I think you might have called her into existence. That Petra was an aberration, someone who didn't exist before she met you. When you decided to throw me out I went from being that girl to the person I had been before you came into my life. The woman you married was so burned up by some—some abnormal passion that she behaved in a way that was totally incongruous.'

He was watching her with the alert purpose she remembered of old, his whole attention focused on her. While she watched something flickered in his eyes, and he smiled, almost knowingly, as though she had suddenly given him the key to some problem hitherto beyond his solving.

'I see,' he said slowly, holding her eyes with a mesmeric intensity that sent a remembered shudder through her. 'Is that how you've justified hiding inside an iceberg? But you can't just extinguish that younger Petra—she existed then, she has a right to exist now.'

She smiled slowly, sadly. 'Sometimes I wonder if she ever did exist,' she said a little forlornly.

'Oh, yes, she existed all right,' he said with a flat conviction more powerful than any histrionics could have been. 'And she had a lot more going for her than you do now; she was no bloodless automaton, going out at night to events that bore her, sleeping with old friends to fill her empty nights...'

Yes, he knew the exact spot to aim for, the tender wound that wouldn't heal. Scarcely aware of the meaning of his words, she pulled away, her face losing colour to present him with a profile as finely outlined as a cameo, and as lacking in animation. She fought a brief, vicious internal battle for control, and was winning, when he swore and moved with a sudden savage swiftness, grabbing her just as she was about to leap out of the bed.

'No, you don't,' he ground out, hauling her back in with such force that she was splayed across his bare chest. 'I'm not going to let you run away. For once in your life, Petra, you're going to recognise what you've done to yourself.'

She was very still, holding herself stiffly against him, feeling the dreaded weakness stealing through her body on soft thief's feet. His flesh burned beneath her. The abruptly recalled textures of hair above satin skin, the sleek, taut swell of muscle and sinew were a torment and an agony.

'Saving me from myself?' she mocked, looking down into the uncompromising contours of his face just to show them both that she could do it, she wasn't afraid of him. 'But I like being the way I am, Caine.' She allowed a sliver of scorn to sharpen her voice. 'I don't need rescuing, I'm quite capable of looking after myself.'

'Leading a bloody sterile life?' he said through his teeth. 'Deliberately choosing safe, barren love-affairs? Were you so traumatised by your mother's total inability to pick the right man that you've taken the opposite path?'

His words struck home as nothing else could have done. But, although she went rigid with pain and humiliation, Petra managed to retort with a soft, icy hauteur, 'I don't have to justify my life or my character to you.'

'What character?' he asked rudely, baring his teeth in a savage smile as she flinched.

Stung, she pushed against him, snapping, 'If you think I've got no personality it's strange that you insisted on marrying me again.'

He controlled her futile attempt to get away with ease, narrowing his eyes so that all she could see were slivers of silver, burnished, opaque, successfully hiding his thoughts. He held her imprisoned against the hard warmth of his chest, and smiled, a slow, cold threat.

'For a moment,' he mused, 'you looked almost alive again. I wonder how long it will take for you to surrender those castle walls and allow yourself to feel something more than a well-bred disdain for the rest of creation?'

Her face assumed that cool, well-bred expression she used as a mask. 'I do not feel any——'

Interrupting, he said, 'Yes, you do. Does it give you some sort of perverse pleasure to pretend that you're a princess in her tower, despising the ordinary mortals who scurry around beneath your patrician little feet? You've managed to convince the world that you're far removed from the messy lives they lead, their inconvenient passions and undisciplined emotions. And when they become importunate you soon put them in their place, don't you? Even your name suits you; Petra, stone. They call you the Stone Princess, and that's the impression you try so hard to give—serene and perfect, and as cold as hell. And that's why you're frightened of me, because I know that's not the real Petra, not the woman who writhed in my arms with passion——'

A sudden hard shove took him by surprise so that she was able to scramble out of the bed without hindrance, her jaw clenched to stop the chattering of her teeth.

So that was why he had insisted on marriage! He wanted to see her once more helpless and humiliated by the power of her desire, at the mercy of the quivering weakness that used to assail her every time she saw him.

In other words, revenge. She would see him in hell first.

Without trusting herself to speak, she walked stiffly through a doorway in the wall, and found herself in a basic bathroom, clean but certainly not luxurious. No sound came from the bedroom. He was probably, she thought viciously, lying in bed smiling with feral pleasure at the thought of her humiliation.

Biting her lip, she stared around, then, impelled by the need to seek solace in ordinary, everyday things, she washed her face. The water was freezing. She was gasping as she dried herself, and reached for her toothbrush. While she performed her ablutions her thoughts scurried round and round, getting nowhere, blocked by the unassailable fact that he had calmly taken over her life and there was nothing she could do about it. The independence she valued so highly was shattered, his brutal intervention revealing it as the fragile façade it was.

Shudders of apprehension caught up with her; head bowed, she grasped the edge of the basin. But almost immediately she straightened and went back into the bedroom, a bath-sheet wound around her, her skin pulled tight by coldness and fear.

'Am I to gather that you have no intention of making this farce of a marriage real until I revert to being "the real Petra"?' Her tone invested the words with far from subtle scorn.

He lay perfectly relaxed in the wide bed, the tawny skin of his broad shoulders a startling contrast to the white percale sheets. He was as lazily satisfied as a beast of prey after a successful hunt; his long limbs were completely relaxed, his expression amused as he surveyed her shuttered face.

'Is that,' he asked in silky insinuation, 'what you want? That we consummate our marriage?' His eyes roamed her tense figure, lingering on the slender length of her legs and the gentle curve of breast and hips.

Tiny rivulets of fire followed the path of that leisurely, insulting survey. Fighting hard to control the sudden weakness that attacked her, Petra said harshly, 'No!'

'My feelings exactly.' Not a hint of emotion in the crisp voice, or the limpid gaze. Behind the long lashes his eyes were fixed on her face, searching for any crack in her armour, the least betrayal by a quivering muscle, probing for her thoughts and reactions beneath the smooth shield of her sophistication.

Petra shuddered, as cold as she had been hot. 'I see. Then why——?' She broke off, hating the mirthless smile that creased his cheeks.

'Why did I insist we marry? Perhaps it was to see just how far you were prepared to go to protect your uncle.'

Apprehension fixed her gaze to his face. Inwardly shuddering, she watched the colourless eyes crystallise into splinters of ice. 'Was that the reason?'

'That's none of your business,' he said indifferently. 'However, I'm not going to trade money and freedom for the delights of your delectable body. I've already been down that road.'

'I wasn't——'

'Offering?' He sounded amused, but there was no warmth in his eyes, not even when they repeated that insolent survey. With a connoisseur's eye he watched unbidden colour scorch up through her skin. 'Just as well, princess, because I'm not buying. When you come to me it will be because you want me, not because you want to save your uncle's bacon.'

'But what is going to happen to him?' She stopped, fighting for control, aware that if she once lost it he would have her exactly where he wanted her. After a short, fierce struggle she forced the bitter anger down.

'I'm not going to do anything to him.'

'You'll just let the debt go?'

He nodded, watching her with the impersonal face of a statue. 'But I'm afraid it's not going to put off the evil day. Stanhope's is doomed.'

She winced, reading the truth of the brutal assessment in his face. 'If the firm goes under it will take the livelihood of a lot of good people with it. In this economic climate I can't see many of them getting jobs again, can you?'

'A pity,' he agreed heartlessly. 'But that's the way things are. Of course, it means that any hopes you had of gaining control of the business are gone.'

'That doesn't matter,' she said absently. 'I didn't expect anything, really.'

'So you knew that the business was in danger?' He spoke softly. 'When did you realise that, princess? When your uncle told you he needed money and suggested you help him get it from me?'

Her hand clenched at her side, but she said nothing, staring at him with a stony expression that hid the panic and the outrage, the flaring, elemental antagonism.

'So much for your protestations of innocence.' He drove his point home with cruel persistence, linking his hands behind his neck as he watched her with the flat, unblinking stare of a predator. He hadn't sounded vindictive, he hadn't even sounded angry. His voice had been completely dispassionate.

When had she realised that Stanhope's was in trouble? He was right; it had been when her uncle had admitted to borrowing the money, first the bridging loan, then the loan that never was from the bank. That had breached the walls of her confidence, and over the years she had relinquished all hopes of a third generation of Stanhopes owning the firm.

'I need some clothes,' she said, staring around the room blindly.

'They're in the wardrobe and the top two drawers in the chest.'

Arms full of the first garments she found, Petra turned and looked at him. 'So you brought me here to indulge in a little revenge,' she stated bitterly.

A smile as sharp and as cutting as a knife-blade made her shiver again. 'Perhaps.'

'I despise you.' The words were like stones.

Caine grinned and let his eyes wander over her thin form, too obvious under the damp towel. Petra felt the sudden heat of colour washing over her, and held the clothes in front of her like a shield.

'Of course you do,' he said softly, getting out of the bed, his lean, naked body taut with energy and good health, the muscles moving and bunching beneath the sleek, satin skin, an aura of power and determination crackling around him. Golden-brown, a burnished predator, forceful with the casual cruelty of his kind. 'It's a start, I suppose.'

Petra gave a horrified choke and ran into the bathroom, his low laughter echoing painfully in her ears.

Dressed in corduroy jeans, a brushed cotton shirt and a jersey, her hair dragged back from her face in an unbecoming knot, Petra stood for a moment staring unseeingly at the white-painted walls, her hands pressed to her pale cheeks. The only sound she could hear was her heart thudding in her chest. Running out of control, a mixture of emotions buffeted her with their intensity, but underneath the fury and the caution, the savage desire for retribution, the fear, she could feel something else—a tiny quiver of attraction.

Caine was ruthless enough to make her pay for her uncle's transgressions. The question was, in what coin?

His references to her mother, and his insistence on keeping their marriage platonic, proved that he despised her for the blatant sensuality she hadn't been able to control during their short marriage. Well, he wouldn't see any signs of it this time, she thought grimly, lifting her chin in a gesture of defiance. She was not going to risk humiliation again.

She was struck by a fresh, unpleasant thought, and her heart stopped. Perhaps he was even more cruelly subtle than she had guessed. Did he hope to make her as emotionally dependent on him as she had been all those years ago? Had the cool mask of her control savaged his ego?

Pain pulled her shoulders forward; she hugged her midriff, struggling to draw breath into her lungs. But no, not even Caine could be that cruel. Straightening up, she collected her thoughts and walked quietly through the small bedroom with her gaze averted from the crumpled bedclothes.

Through another door was a small, clean, old-fashioned and very basic living-room with a wooden table and chairs in one corner against a counter that formed one side of a kitchen. A black wood-fired stove was backed into a corner.

There was no sign of Caine. Petra's breath expelled in hissing relief as she walked across to the old-fashioned double-hung window on one side of the door. A veranda protected the front of the house; one corner was stacked with split manuka logs, and from it steps went down to a yard overgrown with grass and weeds. An old orchard sprawled to one side within a slack fence of rusted wire and crooked battens; through the soft rain Petra glimpsed apples and quinces on the straggly trees, while at the back a citrus tree of some sort was dotted with golden globes. In another corner was a huge sasanqua camellia, the small cerise flowers glowing like jewels through the misty rain.

By an old tree-stump that stood ten feet tall, a relic from the days when fire was used to tame the bush, stood Caine's BMW, totally incongruous in this wild landscape. Apart from that there was nothing but trees and hills, their outlines concealed by drifting misty rain, the stark, hard bones of the land covered in a cloak of second-growth bush.

It was lonely and forlorn, oppressive in its isolation. Why on earth had he bought a holiday-home here? Shivering, Petra turned back to the room with its brightly coloured rugs on the timber floor.

A quick glance into the firebox of the range revealed no sign of flames or embers. If she intended to have a bath at any stage of the day, and certainly if she wanted coffee or anything hot to eat she was going to have to light the wretched thing.

Paper and kindling reposed in a basket close by. Within minutes she had coaxed a flame into life, filled a kettle with water, and set it on the hob to boil.

Of course she was using mundane domestic chores to stop herself from thinking about the situation she was in. She needed breathing space, time to marshal her thoughts.

Her teeth clenched, she stared blindly out of the small window above the sink. Caine had been hard when she first met him, but until the last day of their marriage he had showed her only gentleness. And if sometimes it had been rather condescending at least he had been tender.

But he had not got where he was now by being compassionate and kind. Petra shivered, and poked some more dry kindling into the firebox, her hands trembling. It was terrifying to be the one on the receiving end, with all the force of that implacable, unsparing will bent on her. What exactly did he want from her?

Surrender to her unease would only intensify it. Firming her mouth, she set the table, putting out marmalade and butter, a jug of milk and cups and saucers on to the faded Formica top. A box of muesli on the bench made her swallow compulsively. There was no way she was going to get that down her throat. And, she thought, looking into the firebox for a brief second, no way she was going to be able to make toast in that inferno. Trust Caine to choose a place without electricity as a hideaway!

Checking the cupboards, her eyes became thoughtful as she surveyed the large amount of food, mostly basics and staples, as well as tinned and freeze-dried, that occupied the shelves. Clearly he came here quite often, and intended coming again. How often had he slipped into New Zealand in these past eight years?

She had just poured boiling water into the very modern coffee-plunger when she heard Caine walk up on to the veranda. Instantly unease clutched her stomach. Battling against it, she sliced a small amount of butter into an old, heavy cast-iron pan and put it on the range, ready for the bacon.

He took a few seconds to divest himself of his wet-weather gear out on the veranda, then strode in, carrying the scent of rain and fresh-growing things with him.

'I've been thinking,' he said without preamble.

CHAPTER EIGHT

'YES?'

He hesitated, then said with a crispness that rang slightly untrue, 'We never really got to know each other, did we? Oh, we talked together before we were married the first time, but the fact that we wanted each other just this side of obsession made what we said irrelevant.' His beautiful mouth twisted in a self-derisory smile. 'And after we married we were too busy making love to have any time for conversation. But we're older now, with any luck wiser, and certainly more sensible. And although we are no longer in love with each other——'

'If we ever were,' she interjected, her voice as wry as his.

He stared at her, his expression hardening. Petra shrugged. 'It's a strange sort of love that has no trust,' she finished, choosing her words carefully.

She saw comprehension in his face before he looked past her to the kitchen. 'Something's burning.'

The smell of sizzling butter assailed her nostrils; whirling around, she hauled the cast-iron frying-pan off the hob, gasping as the hot metal scorched her fingers.

Instantly he was beside her, grabbing her hand and turning on the cold tap in one swift movement, then pushing her fingers under the stream of water until the pain had ebbed and she said unevenly, 'It's all right. Look, they're not even going to blister.'

He traced the fading red bar across her skin, his face closed and withdrawn, the arrogant profile stark against the painted walls.

'I'll have to remember to use an oven-cloth,' she said when the silence stretched dangerously between them. He nodded, and with exquisite care dried her hand. The

127

rain drummed down again, a curtain pulled over the stark outlines of hills and trees.

'It's fine,' she whispered into the charged atmosphere, and moved away to wipe out the pan with a paper towel and put in more butter, taking the opportunity to stand with her back to him as she watched the butter spread out across the bottom of the pan. But the impact of his regard burned into her skin as she picked up the tongs and added four rashers of bacon.

'What I was about to say,' he began after a moment, his voice cool and judicial yet with the undertone of determination that infused everything he said, 'is that I intend our marriage should work this time. I think we should try to learn to understand each other, and for that reason I'm prepared to forgo my privileges as a husband until we agree we want to take that final step.'

Sheer, unsuspected disappointment fountained up through Petra, forcing her to realise that some unregenerate part of her, the part that had succumbed so helplessly to his sexual charisma eight years ago, had been waiting with disgusting anticipation for the moment when he took her to bed once more.

So much for her pride in her hard-won strength, her self-sufficiency! Beneath it all she was still a famished adolescent avidly yearning to taste the delights of passion with him once more. Like her mother, she was unable to change.

Shock, and her disgust with herself turned her voice wooden as she replied, 'Yes, all right. That seems sensible.'

A hand on her shoulder turned her to face him. He was looking grim, his expression set, his cutting gaze probing her closed face, the knot of pale ashen hair, the disciplined line of lips that had once been soft and vulnerable. Something wicked gleamed in the depths of his eyes.

'However, don't bank on it lasting for too long. I'm not superhuman,' he warned. Reaching out, he yanked the pins from her hair, letting the soft warm flood of it cascade over his hands.

'I like it better this way,' he said laconically, smiling as she tried to pull away, fear welling up inside her in an irresistible flood when she encountered the icy implacable quartz of his gaze.

His fingers relaxed. Petra moved swiftly out of his reach, grabbing the tongs to turn the bacon needlessly in the pan, realising that she had made a fundamental error.

From the first she had assumed that Caine was the same man who had walked out on her eight years ago. But he wasn't. Perhaps he had never been, perhaps she had always seen him through the rose-coloured spectacles of love, softening his faults in the heat of her need for him.

This Caine—merciless, enigmatic, whose blazing sexuality was at the mercy of his cold, incisive brain, was the real Caine Fleming, and she did not know him at all. She had made the most fatal of errors, allowing her misconceptions to colour her view of the situation.

The satisfying smell of bacon filled the air as she pulled open the egg carton. It was amusing, with a cosmic sort of irony, that she should only now realise what she had done. Unknowingly, hiding it even from herself, she had waited eight years for a man who didn't exist.

Caine was dangerous, a dark, compelling man who wore ruthlessness like a banner. Deftly, without thinking, she broke an egg into the pan, her mind racing around in circles as she tried to work out what she should do next.

Exhaustion was a bruise on her soul. She had been such a fool; she had spent the last eight years transforming herself into the sort of woman she had been sure he wanted, someone cool and controlled, as controlled as he had been with her except on that last, shattering day.

And it had all been for nothing. He didn't love her, he never had, and, no matter how much she remodelled her personality, he was never going to. He wanted her. It was as simple as that—the casual, potent lust of virile man for fertile woman, the instinct that had kept the human race going, and probably caused it more pain and grief than any other. But he was able to control his desire, as she had never been able to control hers.

'What are you thinking?' he asked suddenly.

She looked at him, her face a little pale but otherwise as composed as ever. 'I was wondering why you decided we should get married again.'

His shrewd eyes scanned her down-bent countenance. 'If I want a family it's past time I started on one, and better the devil you know,' he drawled at last. 'And, as I'm no longer enslaved by a conviction that you are young and innocent and pure, I'm not going to suffer the disillusion that sent me halfway across the world when I discovered that you'd betrayed me.'

White-lipped, striving to make her voice as matter-of-fact as his, Petra said, 'I did not betray you. I had no idea what Uncle Laurence was trying to do.'

He lifted his brows, watching the deftness with which she transferred the bacon and egg to his plate. 'Possibly you've said it so many times you even believe it. It doesn't matter any more, Petra. If you'd been happily married when I turned up again I'd have thought no more about it, but as you aren't it seems a good idea for both of us. I want children, don't you? And this time we both know what we're doing. And why.'

'You bastard,' she whispered.

His grin was savage and lethal. 'Merely sensible, princess. I can see no need why we shouldn't have a good marriage. You've learned a few things; eight years ago you couldn't even cook toast. Now you can cope with a wood range.'

'It didn't take much intelligence to work out that if we want hot water we're going to have to keep the range

going, and I was a Girl Guide; I know how to light fires.
As for the cooking——' her voice wavered a little before
regaining its cool deliberation '—what's so difficult about
bacon and eggs?'

'You'd be surprised how hard it is to cook decent
bacon and eggs,' he remarked.

He certainly ate them with enjoyment, raising his
brows when he realised that she was going to eat only a
piece of toast, but making no comment until Petra got
up to pour herself another cup of coffee.

'I'll have one too,' he said, adding with the courtesy
that had been one of the first things she noticed about
him, 'please.'

Of course she remembered how he liked it—almost
black, unsugared—and wondered why the small things
of that marriage were so indelibly fixed in her mind while
the larger ones seemed to have faded. Because they hurt
too much to remember? She had deliberately suppressed
the memories of what it felt like to be in his arms, crazed
with passion, her whole being arching up to the apex of
sensation, lost, drowned in desire and ecstasy.

Heat flooded through her, liquid and totally uncontrollable. The coffee-pot trembled. Biting her lip with
volitionless savagery, she poured out and brought the
cup and saucer across to him, unable to evade his
watchful scrutiny.

'One thing your aunt taught you that I whole-
heartedly approve of,' Caine murmured, the words a
taunt, 'is the old-fashioned art of serving a man.'

Petra replied tonelessly, 'A pity someone didn't teach
you that for every right you claim there is an obligation.'

'Not a feminist, princess?'

'Would appealing to feminism convince you?'

'No,' he said calmly, 'although I have no quarrel with
the main thrust of their argument. I do object to their
beliefs that children have little need of a mother, provided their physical needs are met.'

She lifted her brows. 'I don't think I've read that any-where in the literature,' she commented caustically.

'Then what would you say to the conviction that women are entitled to leave their children with child-minders while they pursue satisfaction in their careers?'

'I'd say,' she returned with spirit, 'that most women have to work nowadays to get any sort of decent standard of living.'

'You're evading the issue, and you know it.' Trading her stare for stare, he leaned back in his chair and said calmly, 'So convince me.'

She didn't know whether she convinced him, partly because she had a sneaking sympathy with his ar-gument, probably derived from the fact that she had spent most of her childhood wanting some sort of at-tention from her mother, even if she had to resort to tantrums to get it, but she argued the question with a crisp common sense that demanded logical answers.

The quick thrust and parry of debate was exhilar-ating. Petra enjoyed sharpening her intelligence, had even attended a discussion group while she had been taking her degree, but this was something else again. Once more she was faced with the full extent of Caine's intelligence, the brilliant depths of a brain more awesomely clever than any she had encountered. Yet, instead of being ex-hausted, she realised as the rain drummed down with redoubled strength that she was invigorated.

If this was what he meant by learning to understand each other she was happy to co-operate, to ignore as best she could the hunger that prowled feverishly through her, setting fire to every cell.

But they had filled the morning with talk, and she had enjoyed it more than she had enjoyed anything for years.

Later, however, making the bed, she wondered how she was going to bear the following days, the frustrating intimacy which she had no way of avoiding short of running out into the rain and losing herself in the bush and the impersonal hills.

She sank down on to the side of the bed, staring unseeingly at the crisp white sheets. The rest of the house might be as basic as they came, she thought distractedly, but the bed was a very luxurious affair indeed, specially built for someone as tall as the man who intended that they share it until he decided they knew each other well enough to make love.

A curious hot shiver snaked down her spine, but she faced the prospect unequivocally. That basic, unabashed attraction was still there; sooner or later she was going to give in to it.

Her calm, serene, ordered life was sliding willy-nilly through her hands, taking every bit of control she had won over it. If he had his way she would once more be dependent on him for her emotional security while he, unbearably detached, remained self-sufficient. That aloofness had rubbed her raw when she was a green girl; it would drive her mad now. Somehow she had to convince him that she had not known of her uncle's plans those long eight years ago! Otherwise their marriage would be a complete sham.

And she was only just beginning to understand how very much she wanted it to work. She was still sitting there, her eyes stretched unbearably in her pale face, when she heard him come back.

Leaping to her feet, she pulled up the duvet and sheets, and set the pillows at the head of the bed. A quick search revealed her nightclothes in one of the drawers. It gave her an odd sliding sensation in her stomach to realise that he had unpacked all her clothes, even the most intimate of them, and put them away. She was picking out the nightgown that was the least revealing when Caine appeared in the doorway, his hair gleaming with moisture, his expression changing to mockery when his glance travelled from the nightgown in her hands to the militant expression on her face.

'I'm sure I put away several much prettier ones last night,' he mocked.

'This is the most comfortable,' she said grimly, fighting back the heat that raced along her cheekbones.

She could hear the taunt in his tone. 'Of course it is, princess. It's all right, I think I can manage to control my lust, even if you do tempt me by wearing any of the frothy bits of nothing I unpacked last night.'

Mouth tight with anger, summoned mainly to banish the empty chill in her heart, Petra snapped, 'I'm sure you can.'

'Of course,' he went on, watching her with ambiguous, translucent eyes, not a sign of emotion warming their measureless depths, 'the same applies to you, doesn't it, princess?'

'Don't call me that!'

'Why not? That's what you are—a stone princess, drifting through the days too afraid to risk your heart in anything but a joyless, long-term, luke-warm affair with Carey. You're afraid to step out from behind the protection of your cosmetics and clothes and exquisite manners, the glossy, seamless shield of your sophistication, because that armour keeps your emotions safely under control. Emotions are messy things, aren't they? You never know what they're going to do, so it's much safer to hide them, repress them, convince yourself that you don't need them. Oh, your aunt trained you well, Petra. But she must have had fertile soil to till, because you wouldn't have got that way just by training.'

Humiliated by the excoriating flick of contempt in his voice, Petra shuddered inwardly. But although her neck was painfully stiff she held her head high as she responded in an even voice, 'If I'm so cold, why did you force me to marry you again? I know it's not just because you want me. I imagine you have wanted many women, but you haven't married any of them.'

He smiled and bent forward to kiss her mouth, his own suddenly hard and heated, forcing her head back. It was agony to keep still, agony to fight back the degrading response that seared through her, but she managed to do it because it would have been greater agony to surrender to it.

'I didn't force you to marry me; there are always choices to be made. And, in spite of the fact that you lied to me eight years ago when you told me you loved me, in spite of the fact that you prostituted yourself for your uncle then and yesterday, I still want you.'

Any triumph she might have felt at his open avowal of desire died as bitter as Dead Sea fruit in her mouth. Absorbed and intent as his face was, with the tell-tale flush of passion across his high cheekbones, his will beat against her like the cold, hard denial of a wall.

Her mouth whispered his name. He rubbed a thumb along her shaking lips, and she had to stop herself from kissing it. Shame and despair struggled for supremacy.

'But when you surrender,' he went on in the same impersonal voice, 'it won't be in payment of a debt, or to fulfil a bargain, but because you can't help yourself.' His fingers were cruel on her chin, and he held her trapped in his unsparing gaze. 'That's what you owe me.'

Cold sweat broke out across her temples. With wide, unfocused eyes she stared into a face rendered demonic by smouldering purpose.

'You're a coward, princess, hiding behind your fortress walls. I'm going to break through that shell you've constructed around yourself. I'm going to smash it down. That's what frightens you, isn't it? The fact that I can make you forget everything your aunt taught you—all the "correct, proper, approved, reasonable" ways to behave. When you accept that in a bed we're not princess and peasant, but just a man and a woman with a need for each other that no amount of good manners can legislate against, we'll start a marriage. Now put on your raincoat, we're going for a walk.'

Resistance, Petra decided, swallowing the bitter dregs of her humiliation as she pulled on her raincoat, shouldn't be too difficult; she had only to remember what the alternative was! An abject, degrading surrender of everything she held important in herself, and the knowledge that even while he was taking her he would despise her.

Strengthened by this reminder, she joined him outside the door, unsurprised to see him in a dark green coat and boots.

The drive, if the pot-holed track could be called that, wound down the side of the hill before disappearing into a clump of second-growth bush. She had no idea how far it was to the road, but she had heard no sound of traffic while she had been there.

Sound didn't travel well in this weather, of course. The low cloud and general dampness in the air muffled it, but if they had been within a mile of a road she would have heard something. Ergo there was no road within a mile, and even if there were it seemed unlikely that there was much in the way of settlement on it. They were definitely in the back-blocks.

'No, not that way,' he said absently. 'We'll head over the hill.'

He strode across the yard, through puddles and past a little shed which held a great pile of logs. Once there had been a fence, but the wires had almost rusted away and the posts were leaning drunkenly at all angles. Misty but penetrating, rain clouded the hills.

Neither spoke as they began to climb through gaunt, sparse tree-trunks blackened by some long-ago fire. The land was certainly not farmed. Manuka bushes were creeping across the paddocks from the edge of the bush, their small, exquisite flowers dusted like snow across the slender grey-green needles of the leaves. Gorse, the curse of Northland, was conspicuous by its absence, although there were some long-dead bushes in the tangled grass.

A native pigeon, big and magnificent with its white breast and green-blue shoulders, flew over, closely followed by another. With an unaccountable lift to her spirits Petra gazed about. Below, perhaps five hundred feet or so down the steep, rough hills was a harbour, thin and fretted by inlets, but no matter how hard she looked she could see no signs of civilisation. No houses, no roads, no boats, not even any animals in the rough pasture.

Petra's heart beat a little more rapidly as she scanned the dangerous, foaming line of breakers across the narrow harbour entrance. It had to be the west coast of Northland, because none of the east coast harbours had bars across them.

'It looks—remote,' she said. The rugged grandeur of the hills and the wild fascination of the coast relegated human preoccupations to their proper insignificance in the cosmos.

'Yes.' Caine stopped and looked around, as untamed as the land and the sea. 'Not a house in sight,' he observed with satisfaction.

Petra looked about, licking the soft salt tang of the air from her lips, taking in deep breaths of the damp, cool caress of the air. To the right the great swell of hills was covered by low, hanging clouds and drifting showers. Bush-covered, mysterious, almost threatening, they glowered down, the occasional dark rock face glistening with moisture.

The track wound on and on, climbing around the steep sides, sometimes almost petering out in clumps of rain-soaked bush, sometimes a scar across a hillside that was still struggling to remain in pasture. Far below the harbour was grey and deserted, the only sign of movement the pattern of rain across its surface and the long line of breakers sheltering it from the savage Tasman Sea.

'You'd wonder why anyone ever tried to farm it,' Petra said quietly.

'Thirty years ago everyone was certain that almost any land could be brought into production.' Caine stopped to follow her gaze around the wild, lonely scene. 'I don't know how many people broke their heart on this before they called it a day.'

'Is it yours?'

He lifted his brows, his face dark and saturnine. 'Yes, it's mine. It was the first thing I bought when I began to make money.'

'A refuge?' she asked, intrigued. During that brief courtship and scarcely longer marriage he had never mentioned the place.

'A place where I can relax. It comes of growing up on a farm, I suppose, the need to own something green and growing, a place where I can look around and see nothing but hills and bush.'

Petra felt as though he had handed her something rare and precious, a glimpse into his soul. 'Most New Zealanders head for the beach.' Trust him to need something different. 'Where do you go in America when you feel the need to get away?'

'There are mountains there, magnificent great peaks. But whenever I have time I come back here.'

So he *had* been back and she hadn't known, hadn't even suspected! And what would you have done if you had known? she asked herself cynically. Not a thing.

'How are your family?' she asked, masking the tentative note in her voice.

The broad shoulders lifted in a swift shrug. 'My parents are well. My brother has his own farm in Te Awamutu, and both my sisters are married.'

'And the Andersons?'

'I'm surprised you remember them.'

She remembered everything he had ever said, but she wasn't going to tell him that.

'They're both dead,' he said calmly.

She touched his arm, felt the muscles clench, and dropped her hand. 'I'm sorry.'

His teeth showed a moment in his smile. 'Don't be, they had a good life. I repaid them every cent they had spent on me, and made sure they never wanted for anything.'

Puzzled by the hint of bitterness, Petra looked up into his face. His expression was shuttered, a teak carving without softness or mercy, the hard eyes hooded.

'Did they want repayment?' she asked quietly.

He smiled, a hard, quick mirthless movement of his mouth. 'Oh, yes,' he said. 'They all wanted repayment. My parents sold me, but they wanted more when they realised how well I was doing. So I bought them a farm, and settled more money on them. Then the Andersons wanted their share. So I repaid them. I bought my brother his farm and gave my sisters an equivalent amount each, as well.'

Sickened, her heart wrung with compassion, Petra ventured, 'Do you see any of them?'

The broad shoulders shrugged. 'Only when they want more. But that's life, isn't it?' He must have seen something in her expression, because he finished cruelly, 'After all, that's why you married me, too.'

And now she knew why he had reacted with such brutality when he believed she had sold herself to him. Petra drew a deep, painful breath. In the light of this revelation his attitude was only too logical! First rejected by his family, then exploited by them.

No, not *exploited*; Caine was too strong to be used by anyone. He accepted their cupidity with a casual disdain that revealed just how little he thought of them, but surely beneath that profound cynicism there had to be pain. And the pain must have been even greater when the Andersons proved corrupt, too.

No wonder he had assumed the worst! No wonder he found it impossible to believe that she had married him because she loved him. Caine had handed over the loan which he thought she had sold herself for with the same cynical contempt that he felt for his family and foster-parents.

Oh, Uncle Laurence, she thought wearily, if you only knew what you were doing when you saw him as a prospect!

'When my mother died a couple of years ago,' she said with simple candour, not really aware why she was telling him this, 'I went to the funeral but I couldn't cry. Nobody else was crying either. It seemed an awful waste of a life, to die and have no one cry for you.'

'What was she like?'

Staring unseeingly out over the harbour, Petra's eyes came to rest on the huge breakers marching in serried rows to smash themselves in a welter of foam against the bar. 'She was—unstable,' she said at last, striving to be objective. 'She needed to be loved, but she made such demands on her lovers that none of them could give her what she hungered for. I don't really know whether she knew what she wanted. She was addicted to love, to romance, and in the end it killed her.'

She brooded silently, remembering the irrational highs and lows, the laughter, the screaming rages, and above all the tears that had marked Anne Stanhope's life. The tears that had rolled down her mother's beautiful face, anywhere, everywhere, the embarrassing shouting matches, the sobs and pleas and demands for forgiveness, for love, for tenderness...

Petra shivered.

'What is it?' Caine asked, watching her with that intent scrutiny, as though he could see right into her soul.

She turned her face away. 'She was like the water out there, unable to do anything but smash herself on to the rocks of her needs, her faults, her passions. She was notorious, a laughing-stock; even I knew that, although I was only a kid. She used to throw scenes, terrible, humiliating scenes, and she didn't care where she was while she was doing it. Yet she was so tragically unhappy. I didn't realise that until I grew up.'

'It's a wonder she managed to attract any lovers,' he observed indolently.

'Oh, she was beautiful,' she said in a cool, level voice. 'Even the last photographs of her, when she was busily drinking herself to death, can't take away from her her beauty. She looked like everyone's idea of the perfect woman, absolutely exquisite. And she wasn't stupid, she was intelligent, she could dazzle with her conversation, and she had the rare gift of turning anything into an occasion, so that everyone enjoyed themselves immensely.'

Caine said, 'So there were good times too.'

'Oh, yes,' she confirmed, smiling a little wistfully as she recalled some of them. 'She took me to the museum once, and showed me the furniture and the ceramics, telling me about the people who made them and used them, making them come alive for me. But we never went again.'

Rain began to fall, spitting on to the grass and their faces. Without discussion they turned back along the track.

'How did you end up with the Stanhopes?'

'Mother wanted to go to Moorea with a lover, and he didn't want me, so she told me I was having a little holiday, and dumped me on them.' Petra's smile darkened into bleakness. 'I was an obstinate, intemperate, undisciplined little termagant with a truly horrific line in tantrums, but Aunt Kath saw through the façade. When my mother turned up again Aunt Kath refused to give me back. There was a messy court case, and when my father said he wanted me to go to Aunt Kath the judge awarded custody to her and Uncle Laurence. It took her a while, but she worked miracles.'

'Did she?' His voice was dry. 'How?'

'Oh, she loved me.' Her voice softened as she remembered. 'She was everything my poor mother was not— gentle, loving, always there for me, consistent and kind. She got a hell-child, and turned her into a human being.'

'Couldn't she have any children of her own?'

'No.' A raindrop ran down her cheek, and she caught it with her tongue. It tasted of life, pure and sweet.

She felt the impact of his gaze, and looked up to catch the gleam beneath his lashes as he watched the artless little movement. Swift coins of colour bloomed in her cheeks, fading as he looked away.

'So you were the child your aunt couldn't have,' he said judiciously. 'The daughter she made over into her own image. Or perhaps stamped with her own impression is a better way to put it. She transformed you into her child.'

His voice was merely thoughtful, but Petra stiffened, squashing the impulse to defend Aunt Kath. He would never understand how much she owed her aunt and uncle. Besides, she could see what he meant, and was fair-minded enough to admit that he had a point. 'Perhaps,' she conceded, after a moment's thought. 'But she gave me much more than she took from me.'

There was perception in his glance, and a certain amount of irony, but he said nothing more, and she, made heartsick by her memories, was quiet until they got to the house.

There, sticky and damp, she said laconically, 'I need a bath,' and disappeared into the bathroom.

Once in the water she looked dispassionately down at her slender form. Her breasts were small and inconspicuous, her face nowhere near as beautiful as her mother's—or Simone's, for that matter. A spasm of jealousy lanced through Petra as she thought of the model's richly passionate face and lush, curved body, the promise of her wilful, laughing sensuality.

It was a pity that she still wanted Caine with every fibre of her being. On a purely physical level she understood why. Something about the lithe lines of his body, the sleek, deadly grace drew her like a magnet.

Yet she was fascinated by his mind; in the past eight years she had managed to forget that, carefully convincing herself that it was only his body she craved. But their discussion that morning had revealed the forbidden pleasure of matching wits with him, trying to fathom the depths of that cold, incisive intellect, measuring her arguments against his.

A mind in a billion, some fulsome journalist had once said. The writer had not exaggerated.

How could his family have been so—callous? She had been shocked when he'd said they'd sold him, but she had to admit that he had been right. How much it must have hurt him, made him see himself as just another commodity to be bartered for material gain. No wonder he had assumed she had done the same!

Wincing, she splashed water across her breasts. His parents' greed was bad enough, but when the Andersons had made it obvious that they expected to be paid for their help he must have been cut to the quick, wounded in some hidden, vulnerable spot so badly that he had never really recovered.

She was still frowning when she got out of the bath and wrapped the bath-sheet around herself. Her new insight into his attitudes didn't really change anything. He was still the same obdurate autocrat. And she was the same love-sick schoolgirl who had seen him across a moonlit garden and lost her heart permanently.

All he wanted from her was his revenge. Oh, he might be trying to convince himself otherwise, but she knew better. He had married her to prove that he could control the desire that lay coiled like the snake around an apple tree. She had every right to be terrified, because Caine was ruthless enough to do it.

The past years had taught her that she could cope with anything, and hide her feelings while she did it. But this was a matter of survival.

Dressed and back in the kitchen, she put some more wood into the stove, then stood looking out of the window at the sullen sky. The room seemed stuffy yet damp, hemming her in. She went outside on to the veranda, and stood for a moment staring around, her eyes almost wild, all their blue colouring replaced by a sheer, turbulent green.

But losing control wasn't going to help. Taking three deep breaths, she slid her feet into her gumboots, and strode through the puddles to the huge camellia tree by the fence. Its delicate burgundy blossoms looked like something painted on to a Japanese screen, the rain-drops trembling on the silken petals, stamens at the centre of each flower like thin gold wire. Petra had almost reached the tree when she heard a flat *thunk thunk thunk* from the shed.

Swivelling round, she wondered what on earth Caine could be doing. Curiosity got the better of her, and she made her way through more puddles to the shed.

Stripped to the waist, he was using a large axe to chop through great rounds of tree-trunk. Petra's mouth dried. Cool, muted light flowed over the lean contours of his torso, picking out with loving precision the flow and play of golden-brown skin, the tension and force implicit in sleekly muscled arms and wide, flexed shoulders, the sheer masculine strength and skill as the axe was swung high then centred exactly where he wanted it to go, so that it split each round in two.

Petra swallowed, unable to move as the splendid sym-metry of his body played its part in reducing a fearsome heap of logs to neat chunks of wood entirely suitable for the range.

He bent, picking up two of the logs with an easy motion and scooping them on to a pile beside him. In spite of the dank air he was sweating, the sheen of moisture picking out each polished swell of muscle, his latent power given rhythmical expression with every rise and fall of the axe.

Dry-mouthed, Petra turned away. As she picked her way across the yard she concentrated hard on the dainty flowers of the camellia, but it was too late. She could only see the well-oiled strength and co-ordination of the man who split the wood with such elemental satisfaction.

Back in the house she arranged several blooms in a drinking glass, and piled some more wood on the fire. Not only did she have to cook lunch, but he would be needing a shower or a bath when he came in. Firmly repressing the inconvenient memories that teased sensuously through her mind, she filled a large saucepan with water, setting it on the range. She had discovered a packet of brown rice, and decided to cook what her aunt called Spanish Rice, although as it had bacon and cheese in it it didn't sound very Spanish to her!

Within twenty minutes the partly cooked rice had been mixed in with the fried bacon and onions, herbs and a can of tomatoes added, and the whole set to simmer. Petra assembled a salad, washing lettuce and green peppers and tomatoes; close by, the two halves of an avocado had been sliced into pale green crescents ready for garnishing.

Ironically amused by the flowers glowing in the middle of the table, the cheerful red and white checked cloth, winking silver, the delicious smells of food, she listened to the sudden silence that meant Caine had stopped chopping. How easy it was to slip into the old-fashioned way of doing things, with Caine out doing the hard, physical labour while she, in her 'proper' place in the kitchen, prepared food for him!

Another shower deposited its burden, rain splattering across the puddles, thrumming softly on the iron roof. The sulky sky showed no sign of relenting.

A rattle outside denoted the arrival of an armful of wood on to the pile already there. By the time Caine had shucked off his gumboots and come inside Petra was standing by the range, pretending that the Spanish Rice needed her attention.

'Smells good,' he observed as he came in.

'It'll be ready in about twenty minutes,' she said, willing her voice not to sound defensive.

He came over and turned the tap above the sink on, holding a glass beneath the stream of water. Swallowing, she kept her head low and concentrated on the smooth movement of the wooden spoon in her hand. The savoury smell should have filled her nostrils, but she discerned another—the scent of masculine effort, astonishingly evocative.

Go away, her mind screamed silently, and when he'd drained the glass of water he did.

'I'll be ready in a few minutes,' he called over his shoulder as he went into the bedroom.

Petra waited until he was in the shower before she put the spoon down and stood for a moment with her hands clenched on to the edge of the bench. After a short time they stopped trembling.

It was, she thought staring blindly out of the window, going to be damned hard to keep her self-control, but she was not going to give him the pleasure of seeing her come apart. For her own survival she had to convince him that she could control her helpless reaction to him.

When he had demolished a large plateful of the Spanish Rice he complimented her on the food, adding, 'I'll cook dinner.'

'Can you?'

'Oh, yes, I'm a reasonably competent cook. Quite house-trained, in fact.' He looked across at her plate, only half filled, and still far from empty. 'Weren't you hungry?'

She snapped, 'I'm not a big eater.'

And wondered why she was disturbing their tenuous, unnegotiated truce. Of course, it was a defence mechanism. She had been too profoundly affected by the sight of him chopping the wood! His confidence in her eventual capitulation now seemed ominously justified; she had to impose some sort of barrier between them.

'Nonsense,' Caine said with a narrow, mocking smile. 'Eat up, you're too thin as it is.'

'Why don't you say scrawny?'

He responded to her sweet, patently false smile with a slow, clinical assessment that brought quick, shaming colour to her skin. 'I think you're being a little hard on yourself,' he decided at last, still keeping up the pretence of judiciousness. 'You're far from scrawny. And I prefer my women slender. But not skinny. Eat up.'

A small red flicker of temper compelled her reply. 'I'm not hungry.'

'Yes, you are, you're just being bloody-minded. Either you eat, princess, or I make you.'

Her eyes flew to meet his. Naked aggression was a steady glitter in the clear depths of his eyes, combined with a steely determination. If she held out there was no way he could make her eat—and yet . . .

Sullenly, she yielded. 'Very well, although I find it difficult with you watching my every movement.'

'Then I'll make a pot of tea,' he said calmly, getting to his feet. 'But you clear that plate, Petra.'

Which she did, congratulating herself that her instinctive defences had worked. He had pulled in the reins with abrupt brutality, and she could dislike him again.

'Don't sulk,' he ordered with cool effrontery as he brought the tea-tray back to the table.

Petra lifted the mug to her mouth, but her trembling hand made tiny cat's-paws of ripples over the surface of the liquid, so she put it down again.

'Come and play chess with me,' he continued, 'and for a while we can forget that we don't like each other very much.'

She looked down into the tea, her mind working furiously. Naturally he wanted to keep her as sweet-tempered as possible. It would be much easier if he found a docile woman in his arms rather than a wildcat intent on preserving her virtue. And behaving with some degree of compliance might also lull his suspicions and bring about that moment of absent-mindedness she waited for. Without the strength to beat him, she was left only with cunning.

So she said with the right amount of reluctance, 'All right.'

He sent her a slow, teasing smile that made her unruly heart beat high in her throat.

CHAPTER NINE

CAINE won at chess, but Petra came out on top in two hard-fought games of Scrabble, and they evened out in the hands of poker they played. The rain was still pouring down, so he took up a book, and she riffled through the pile of magazines on the bottom of an old bookshelf. Although a couple of years old, they were better than nothing.

She found a ferocious cryptic crossword in one, and settled down to do it, muttering to herself as she filled in the squares. Outside the rain settled down to a steady monotonous drumming. It was an oddly domestic scene, tranquil, almost soothing. The sort of scene, she thought acidly, that made stupid people wonder how things might have been...

Towards evening Caine got up from his impressive tome and began to assemble dinner, clearly at home as he moved lithely around the inconvenient, cramped kitchen. From beneath lowered lashes Petra watched his broad back, and asked herself jealously who had been the last woman he had brought here.

As if she cared! She went back to her crossword, frowning as she struggled to decipher one particularly fiendish clue.

'Wine,' Caine said, putting down a glass of white wine in front of her.

Startled, she looked up.

'One glass won't hurt you,' he said, forestalling her automatic refusal.

Still she hesitated, and he commented, 'I notice that you nurse one glass all evening. Is it because your mother was an alcoholic?'

'Yes.' Her shoulders moved uneasily.

'I doubt if you need to worry,' he said drily as he went back to the kitchen, from which delicious smells were emanating. 'If anything you're too controlled.'

Which sounded odd coming from him. Could anyone be *too* controlled? But Petra didn't ask the question out loud, contenting herself with an eloquent quirk of her brow.

Dinner was excellent, steak Diane served with scalloped potatoes and green beans, followed by cheese and biscuits and fruit accompanied by delicious coffee. Mindful of the contretemps over luncheon, Petra ate manfully. She noted that, like her, Caine was abstemious, drinking only one glass of wine.

By then it was completely dark. The room was filled with a faint hissing noise and the lingering scent of kerosene from the lamps. It should have been unpleasant, but it was—cosy, Petra supposed with a faint grimace.

Pretending to be concentrating, she filled in another clue, very conscious that soon she was going to have to share a bed with the man who lay stretched out on the only other armchair, his dark, arrogantly poised head bent over his book. Her skin tightened, and although it was still raining she was sure she could hear the steady rhythm of his breathing across the room.

When he put his book aside and announced, with a half-hearted yawn, 'Time for bed,' she couldn't prevent a swift, wary glance in his direction, and shivered at the narrow, mocking smile he sent back. He knew just what she was thinking. Reluctantly she got to her feet, her stomach knotted into cramps.

'You have first go at the bathroom,' he said.

Pride kept her back straight and her shoulders high as she walked across the room.

After washing and cleaning her teeth she defiantly donned the nightgown. High-necked and long-sleeved though it was, it was still transparent enough to reveal the slender lines of her legs and body. Setting her mouth, she pulled on a pair of pants. Since they were sketchy satin briefs they would serve merely as a psychological barrier, but they were better than nothing.

Militantly geared for an argument, she was irritated when Caine merely lifted a taunting eyebrow at her on his way into the bathroom. Petra climbed into the bed, and hauled the bedclothes over her. Rigid, so tense that she thought she might snap, she clamped her eyes shut. She heard him come back into the room, the rustle of clothing, the sound of the rain on the roof, then silence.

Cautiously she opened her eyes a slit.

He was standing naked in front of an open drawer, looking down into it. Petra's heart gave a violent lurch, and desire stole like a sickness through her body. She lay without breathing. Then, extinguishing the flare of lust, came fear. Had he lied to her? Did he intend to take what he must realise she would give, if not at first, as soon as he turned the heat up?

The wash of light from the lamp in the bathroom outlined his lean, powerful body in an aureole of gold. Petra swallowed, afraid that the tiny sound could be heard in spite of the rattle of the rain on the iron roof.

She heard the faint slide of the drawer's runners, the soft sounds of his footsteps as he went through into the living-room. There was a click, and the sound of a lamp being blown out.

She opened her eyes tentatively. It was pitch dark so she couldn't see him, but she sensed his approach, and the motion of the springs under his weight didn't surprise her.

Stiff, her pulse thundering in her ears, she lay waiting, ready to repel any advance to the utmost of her effort.

'Goodnight, princess,' he said softly into the darkness, and rolled away from her.

Slowly, so carefully that he couldn't tell what she was doing, Petra turned her head. By then she had her night vision, and she could see the contours of his body, the hump of his shoulder, the darkness of his head on the white pillow.

Stupid, hot, wasted tears welled up, clogging her throat, hurting behind her eyes.

It took her a long time to get to sleep, time spent listening to the rain on the roof, and pondering bleakly on the supreme ironies of life, but eventually she managed it. When she woke it was to warmth, and a sweet helplessness, and the wonderful sensation of being protected from anything the world could throw at her.

Sighing, she nuzzled into heated skin, its satin texture intriguingly netted with fine hair that tickled the sensitive skin of her face. With the tip of her tongue she tasted salt and the intense flavour of masculinity. She smiled when his chest rose sharply at the little caress. In addition, the heart beating heavily against her ear picked up speed, and she smiled again, the blind, sensual smile of a woman in love.

And then she froze. Her lashes flew up.

Caine was looking down at her, his face set in the lineaments of passion, the pale grey eyes darkening perceptibly, a flush along his cheekbones, while she, lulled by sleep, lay bonelessly against the hard tension of his body, the heat and power of his arousal.

'No,' she breathed, pushing against him with a strength that took him by surprise.

'Yes, by God,' he said between his teeth, his hands hard and hurtful as they dragged her back.

Shame sealed her eyes shut, but that only reinforced the signals her other senses were sending her, the sharp scent of aroused male, the tactile pleasure of skin as warm and smooth as silk left in the sun, the surge of honeyed fire through her body, enervating yet urgent, weakening her will, inciting her to surrender, to become a slave to the desire he roused in her.

'I won't make love with you,' Petra said through gritted teeth.

'You have been for the last ten minutes.'

She responded to his implacable tone with dismayed fear. 'I was asleep.'

'Not so sleepy that you didn't know what you wanted,' Caine retorted harshly.

She gave a half-sob. 'I don't want to make love!'

'What the hell is the matter with me?' he snarled, and, at her astonished stare, elaborated starkly, 'You have no objections to going to bed with David Carey. Why not me, for God's sake? And don't tell me you don't want me, because I know you do. You spent all night thrashing around and moaning, and this morning you turned over and fitted yourself into my arms with no hesitation at all. And if you want any further proof——' he ran a casual, insulting hand over the tips of her breasts, which were straining against the thin material of her nightgown '—you've got it here. And here.'

The same insulting hand made a ruthless sweep the length of her body, forcing her legs apart to slide beneath the useless protection of the flimsy satin briefs and probe into the layered centre of her womanhood.

A guttural sound forced its way through her clenched teeth. Her body arched into his hand, and for a hideous moment she almost yielded, aching for fulfilment, shaking with hunger.

'Yes,' he murmured, his voice gravelly with satisfaction, 'you're desperate for me, aren't you? And God knows, princess, I want you just as much.'

If she allowed anything more to happen she would give in. *She couldn't do it.* He despised her enough already; she would die if she looked into his eyes and read there contempt for a woman who couldn't control her sexual urges.

She had seen men look at her mother like that, with a mixture of concupiscence and scorn.

'No,' she gasped, tearing herself out of his arms, and bolting into the bathroom. There was no lock on the door, but she leaned against it, trembling, caught in the grip of a frustration so intense that she had to clench her jaw to keep from crying out.

She heard movement through the door, and caught her breath, staring desperately around for some avenue of escape.

A constant drip on to the floor by her feet caught her attention; she looked up at the ceiling, and thought hysterically, Saved by the rain! For the ceiling bulged ominously. Jerking the door open, she called, 'Caine, the ceiling's leaking.'

His eyes followed hers; he swore and grabbed a pair of jeans and a shirt, dragging them on as he told her to find a bowl, then put a chair under the hatch into the roof in the kitchen.

Barefoot, he disappeared outside, returning after a few seconds with a hammer and tool-kit. Without exchanging a word with her he climbed on to the chair, pushed up the trap-door, and hauled himself up into the ceiling.

'The bowl,' he snapped, extending a hand through the trap-door.

Petra handed up the gaudy plastic thing, and went back into the bathroom to stare anxiously at the bulge. Her lips straightened into a grimace as she realised it was getting bigger. It wouldn't have been quite so bad if it had been over the bath, but of course it wasn't. Poking her head into the bedroom, she realised that the bulge extended into there, over the head of the bed. If the water broke through the bed would be saturated. Outside the rain drove steadily down.

She grabbed the bed and tried to push it away, but it was far too heavy for her to move. She looked upwards, biting her lip, wondering if the wretched bulge really had grown bigger, or whether it was her imagination. The bedclothes lay tangled together; heat scorched up through her skin in mute witness of the fact that she had no self-discipline at all. She had to get away!

Above her she could hear the sounds of Caine's progress across the rafters. Moving quietly, she flew across to the wardrobe and found the trousers he had been wearing the day before.

There was nothing in the pockets, no keys.

Disappointment rose like bile in her throat. Then her eyes narrowed. Silently, barely breathing in case it gave her away, she tiptoed across to his side of the bed, and slid her hand under the pillow that still bore the imprint of his head.

Nothing. Without giving herself time to think she tried between the mattress and the base. And struck gold. Her eyes lit up as she dragged out the car keys.

Yet even as she stole quietly through the house she had to fight the instinct that tried to persuade her to stay, to fight for her love. By the door she paused, torn unmercifully between her head and her heart. It was the memory of his voice saying scornfully that she had slept with David that sent her racing across the yard, the keys clutched in her hand.

Another night like the last one would see her defences fall to her treacherous body's needs. And she could not face it, the triumph in his face when she moaned with shameful ecstasy in his arms, the mask of control ripped from her face forever. He valued her physical surrender only as a means of satisfying his urgent male needs, of proving that she was no better than her mother, reduced to the same helpless sexuality, driven to search for love in the arms of men who despised her.

Nothing could be worse than that. Not even running away.

With a shiver she unlocked the driver's door and slid into the seat, her eyes fixed with wide terror on the door of the house. Her hand shook as she fitted what looked to be the correct key into the slot and turned it.

Success! The engine caught, faltered, making her heart stop, then caught again and settled down to run smoothly. Petra didn't waste time putting the seatbelt on; she didn't even look behind her as she took the big car as fast as she dared through the open gate and down

the narrow, rutted track, high on a wild elation that ran
through her blood like fine old brandy. She had out-
manoeuvred him!

There was no wind, just solid sheets of water filling
the ruts and potholes, making the mud ten times more
difficult to drive through. Hands clenched on the wheel,
eyes straining through the murk, Petra slid more or less
under control down the hillside.

But around one particular corner a mass of greenery
barred the track. Gasping, she stamped automatically
on the brakes and put the car into a sideways skid that
ended up with a resounding thud against the bank.

The force impelled her forward; she hit her head on
the windscreen almost hard enough to put herself out,
but straightened up immediately, staring through the
tangled mass of vegetation. With a low moan she realised that even if she manoeuvred the car out of the
ditch she was not going to be able to get through.
Brought down by the rain, the tree blocked the way
completely, roots and trunk barring the rutted track, the
foliage and branches extending out over quite a steep
drop.

She was still crouched in the front seat, her head on
her arms on the wheel, when, almost immediately it
seemed, Caine wrenched open the door. Rain spattered
her face, and she turned her head, opening reluctant eyes.

She almost cowered. Oh, God, he was furious. She
remembered that look, although she had only seen it
once before, the evening he had come home and de-
nounced her as a treacherous little whore, selling her
favours for money.

'Are you all right?' he demanded in a voice like molten
steel.

She nodded, wincing a little as the incautious
movement reminded her that she had hit her head quite
hard. In spite of his fury his fingers were gentle as they
probed about the tender bruise on her forehead.

'It's all right,' she said weakly, dazed but pliant.

'You stupid little bitch!' She flinched, but he took a deep breath, re-imposing control on his temper. 'Are you hurt anywhere else? Your shoulder? Your ribs?' As he spoke he ran a careful, purposeful hand over the areas he listed.

'No,' she replied dazedly. 'It was just my head, and it wasn't too bad. It didn't knock me out.'

He helped her out, stripped the coat from his shoulders to sling around hers. As he buttoned it he said, 'I can't move the car, I'll need a tractor to pull the tree away, so we'll have to go back. Is that all right?'

'Yes, of course it is.' Indeed, the fresh rain on her face banished the lingering remnants of her lethargy.

Docilely, her head thumping, she stood as he finished the last button, but when he lifted her she said huskily, 'I can walk.'

'Don't be silly.'

Striding with unnatural strength up the slippery drive, he shielded her as much as he could from the driving rain.

By the time they got back to the house Petra was exhausted and completely chastened, wondering bleakly what on earth had persuaded her to steal his car and run away. An icy chill burgeoned from her heart, enveloping her in its grip. She stole a look at his grim visage. No, she could expect no mercy there.

'Get into the bathroom,' he ordered, when they were inside.

Petra shook her head. 'You're colder and wetter than I am. You have the first bath.'

He said with a soft snarl, 'Do you want me to undress you myself?'

'No!'

'Then get under the shower.'

It was clearly useless to argue with him. Without a word she turned and went through the bedroom. A quick glance revealed that the bulge in the ceiling was still there, although it was no longer growing. Apparently he had had time to put the bowl under the leak.

Mouth twisting in mimicry of a smile, Petra sat down on the edge of the bath. A tentative hand revealed that the bump on her head was tender, although the headache was fading; she flinched as she probed at it, her eyes hunted.

Well, she had done it, and he was furious; the only way to deal with the situation she had got herself into was to keep calm and retain her dignity.

But when, clad only in trousers, he appeared in the doorway, dignity was the last thing on her mind. Dry-mouthed, she stared at him, her eyes travelling slowly over the gleaming torso where dark hair curled crisply in a pattern as old as humankind.

'Get in,' he commanded, his voice rigidly distant.

'I'm just about to,' she said meekly as she got to her feet. Of course she would have to stumble. Caine caught her before she realised she had gone, his arms contracting about her thin form, jerking her against him.

For a moment her cheek lay against his chest, her body supported in a grip as strong as a vice. Sensations screamed through her even as she pulled herself away, whispering, 'Thank you.'

'Leave the door open,' he ordered.

Opening her mouth in indignant protest, Petra looked up into eyes like quartz, impervious, defying her to continue her objections. 'All right,' she said, trying hard to see it as a sop to common sense and not a surrender.

A totally humourless smile curved his mouth. 'That's my princess,' he remarked offensively. 'Lacquered and poised and gracious, even after crashing my car.'

Disdaining to give him the satisfaction of a reply, she waited for him to leave, her face studiously impassive, her back held straight enough to hurt her shoulders. She couldn't relax the muscles even after he had left.

The shower did that, soothing her purely physical tension while doing little for the mental strain. Recalling that he too was cold, she washed as quickly as possible, although when she had finished she stood for a moment with her eyes closed in sybaritic pleasure as the water ran down her face, almost able to block the coming confrontation from her mind. The abrupt cessation of the spray brought her lashes wide open. A lean, strong hand, barbarically dark against the white walls of the shower, turned the tap off.

She commanded indignantly, 'Get the hell out of here!'

'Petra,' he said quite gently, 'don't push your luck. There's a doctor waiting in the bedroom——' Her head jerked up so swiftly that she winced, and he finished harshly, 'And if you don't get out immediately I'll pull you out myself!'

The doctor was young, and amused by Caine's arrogant demand for his services. 'Fortunately,' he said, as he examined her, 'I wasn't too far away. I hold a clinic about ten miles down the road, and I was only a few hundred metres from your gate when your husband started harassing my nurse. Got my shoes wet walking up the hill, though.'

Caine had showered and was back in the bedroom by the time the doctor had finished his thorough survey. Petra's eyes travelled from the smoothly handsome face of the doctor to Caine's autocratic, harshly delineated countenance; she could read nothing there.

'How is she?' he asked after a swift, impersonal survey.

The doctor replied calmly, 'I'd say she's come out of it remarkably well. A bump to the forehead, that's all.'

'Shouldn't she have an X-ray?'

The younger man lifted his brows. 'I don't think it's necessary, but if it will make you feel any happier I can ring through to the hospital.'

Huskily Petra said, 'It's not necessary.'

But Caine ignored her, speaking directly to the doctor. 'I'd like you to do that.'

And he was adamant, so, in spite of her protests and the doctor's reassurance, she was taken by the helicopter Caine had summoned somehow to the small hospital standing on its hill overlooking Kawakawa, where she was X-rayed and eventually pronounced fit, with no signs of a fracture or concussion.

Caine was gentle but remote, the cool grey of his eyes oddly opaque. Petra preferred him angry, mocking, anything but this impersonal kindness, the sort he would show to a stranger. When they left the hospital the hired helicopter was still waiting.

'Where now?' she asked in a dazed voice.

'Auckland. I'm taking you home.'

Almost immediately shock and exhaustion tipped her into a sleep that lasted until they were coming in to land.

In Auckland the twin harbours were grey, the city and the islands crouched beneath a pall of rain. Petra watched with incurious eyes, her lashes drooping to keep out the light, for by this time the headache had settled in, and the light made her wince. She shivered. Instantly Caine's arm tightened around her. She lay where she was, drawing strength from his solid, masculine warmth as they landed on top of one of the tall buildings in the centre of the city.

Men with umbrellas rushed out, and Caine set her back in her seat. He got out, and came around, holding out his arms.

'I can get down by myself,' she protested.

His teeth showed in a mirthless smile. 'Humour me,' he said, but it was an order.

Petra bit her lip, but let herself be carried into the building and down the elevator to the basement car park. The men with them were alert but silent; she could feel their curiosity like a palpable force around her. She had never really considered Caine's position as the head of a huge corporation, but the respectful atmosphere, as well as the ease with which he had organised her arrival in Auckland, made her realise now that he was an extremely powerful man, and that he wore that power with an effortless ease.

The Caine she knew and the Caine Fleming, head of a billion dollar industry, were one and the same person, but she knew only one side of him.

Loved only one side of him.

Her head throbbed unmercifully, preventing her from thinking clearly. Once in the big chauffeur-driven car that waited for them in the basement, she leaned back and closed her eyes. Caine stood for a moment outside, his voice clear and incisive as he gave orders then got in and gave her address to the man behind the wheel.

He carried her inside and up the stairs into her white, femininely romantic bedroom, and stripped her efficiently, finding a nightgown in the dressing-room and switching on the electric blanket. The room was dank and chilly, permeated by the sound of the rain on the roof and the windows.

'Here,' he said when she was beneath the blankets. He offered her a glass of water and a pill. 'It will stop that headache.'

Her automatic nod made her wince again as she took the pill. When he turned to go, she said huskily, 'I'm sorry.'

'What for?'

'Crashing the car.'

'The car is nothing,' he said quietly. 'Don't worry about it, it's not badly damaged. Get some sleep now.'

When she woke the curtains were drawn and the heater from the sitting-room had been plugged into the socket so that the room was warm and dry. Petra stretched, rubbing her fingers lightly over her forehead and grimacing when she felt the bump. It was very tender, and probably, she thought ruefully, all the colours of the rainbow by now.

But at least her headache was gone.

She yawned and turned over, her lashes flicking up with astonishment as she saw Caine in the armchair beside her desk, his dark head bent over a book. He looked up, a slight smile softening the saturnine darkness of his face. 'Ah, you're awake. Do you feel better?'

'Yes, the headache's gone.' Confusion made her stupid. 'What are you doing here?'

But he didn't tell her that as her husband he had every right to be in her bedroom. 'Making sure that you're all right.'

She looked astonished, and the smile became grim. 'After all,' he said softly, 'I frightened you into that break for freedom.'

'So you feel responsible?' It hurt in some obscure way. 'It was my decision,' she asserted on a wry note.

'Why did you run?'

She lay watching him, the way the lamp sheened his hair with fire and emphasised the ruthless physical magic that was exclusively his. Perhaps the shock of the near brush with death had clarified her mind, or perhaps it was the lingering traces of the very strong painkiller the doctor had prescribed, but she knew she had to tell him the truth.

'I was afraid,' she murmured.

His brows drew together over the arrogant blade of his nose. 'That I would hurt you?'

'Oh, no!' She sat up, pushing the tangled tresses back from her face with trembling fingers. 'No.'

She would have to tell him, the most secret part of her was going to be exposed. In a voice that was strained yet determined she revealed, 'I was afraid because I wanted you. It was going to start all over again.'

'It was what we both wanted,' he said, watching her with unblinking intensity. 'In spite of my attempts to convince both of us that we needed to learn to know each other we both knew that it wouldn't take much to tip us over the edge. What is there to be afraid of in that?'

Petra's tongue stole out to dampen her arid lips. Her fingers pleated the sheet as she looked away from the man who sat so still, watching her with a guarded expression. In a dull voice she began, 'I've told you a little about my mother, but not—everything. She was a hysteric, a woman completely at the mercy of her emotions. She drove my father away with her jealous demands and her dependency, and when he left she led a life of messy emotional trauma until eventually the lovers stopped coming and she took to the bottle to supply what was lacking in her life. In a lot of ways I was the adult in that household. I loved her—and yet I despised her, and I knew that most other people did too. What I didn't tell you was that although I loved the calm, ordered, serene life my aunt and uncle gave me, the consistency and the love, I suppose I've always felt that I deserted my mother.'

He made a small sound, and she nodded, carefully keeping her eyes averted, her voice even and uninflected as she chose her words. 'Children's logic is brutal, and difficult to withstand. Aunt Kath was very watchful, picking up on any small thing that might have led to the sort of melodramatic excitability my mother was prey to. Any abandonment to emotion, any extremes of temper, even joy and grief, were gently but firmly discouraged. My aunt and uncle loved me, and I loved them, so to please them I learned to control myself, and whether that was what they intended or not I learned that to be controlled was infinitely more important than anything else, far more important than surrendering to happiness or grief, elation or despair. I think Aunt Kath really believes that there is something vulgar about strong emotion. It was a lesson I learned very well.'

'In other words,' he said quietly, 'she did her best to turn you into a copy of herself, expunge everything of your mother, and make you over in her own image.'

Without looking at him she nodded. 'Yes. You were right. But to be fair, Caine, my mother's example was not the one you'd want for your child.'

'Possibly not, although your mother must have had the virtues of her faults, too. You say you were passionate and wilful as though they were vices. But they can be virtues, too.' He shrugged, his gaze as keen as a steel blade as he watched her. 'Most of our reformers have been passionate and wilful. The world would be a much worse place without the legacy of people like Florence Nightingale. Character traits shouldn't be corrected out of existence, no matter how high the motives. By so sweetly, kindly, ruthlessly transforming you, your aunt was making it clear that she loved you on her conditions only. You had to conform to her ideas of the perfect child.'

'Ah, no,' she protested. 'She has always loved me.'

'There is no tyranny like love.' His voice was harsh and curt.

Petra began to object, and he interrupted with a brusque, 'All right, perhaps I'm too cynical. Leave it for the moment. Go on with what you were trying to tell me.'

Clinging unconsciously to the refuge of the bed, her expression remote and cold as she marshalled her thoughts, Petra summoned the words to explain her actions, wondering if she really understood the reasons herself.

'When I met you all the restraint, the control, the self-discipline flew out the window. I was ashamed of myself, embarrassed by the way I felt, the way I behaved with you. I wanted to be controlled, sophisticated. But I couldn't.' Painful colour stung her cheeks. 'When we made love I behaved like the little sensualist you called me, lusting like an animal in heat, and I couldn't help it; I couldn't control my response even though I knew you must despise me for it. I had regressed, I was just like my mother.'

'Oh, God,' Caine said quietly, getting up to pace across to the window. He stopped, staring out into the night.

Petra's eyes clung helplessly to the broad sweep of his shoulders, the tight, male muscles revealed as his fingers drove into his pockets. Biting her lip, she hurried on before her nerve gave way completely. 'So I wasn't really surprised when you came home eight years ago and said it was all over. I'd been expecting it all along, that you'd get disgusted with me and leave. Because that's what her lovers always did...'

'God!' Caine exclaimed in a voice of such molten rage that she flinched. 'Between the lot of us we screwed you up good and proper, didn't we? Your poor mother, the bloody con-job your aunt and uncle did on you, dampening down all that lovely spirit, and me, somehow making you believe that the passion I revelled in was disgusting. Is that why you thought I left?' He swung round to stare at her.

Unable to speak, she nodded, her hands clenched into the soft percale of the sheet.

'Listen to me,' he said, coming across to the bed and inexorably lifting her face to meet his gaze. She began to shake, and he made a muffled sound and sat down, gathered her gently into his arms, and held her until the rigors eased.

Then he said deeply, 'Your passion, the lust you speak so disparagingly of, was one of the reasons I couldn't get you out of my mind, out of my life. You know I was no virgin when I met you, but no other woman has ever been able to give me what you gave me—complete ease of body and soul, a passion so sweet and fiery and generous that I lost myself entirely in it. It didn't disgust me, it didn't make me think that you were anything like your poor, tragic, neurotic mother.'

He held her a little away, compelling her to meet his eyes, centred with blazing pinpoints of light. 'Do you believe me?' he asked softly.

At first hesitant, Petra realised that she did. Slowly she nodded.

'You were the sweetest thing I had ever seen,' he went on thickly. 'Funny and quick, intelligent and compassionate and loving, and I wanted you this side of madness. I still want you like that. If you honestly believed that I found your lovemaking disgusting, then you must have felt the same way about mine. Did you?'

The ice in his eyes was melting, the shards splintering into flickers of fire. Stretching out an imperative hand, he caught a tear that brimmed and fell, and lifted it to his mouth. Petra's slender body caught fire from the fire in him, the path of his gaze scorching a pathway of flame and sensation across her tender skin.

'No,' she breathed. 'Never.'

'Until I saw you again at the racecourse I'd forgotten how beautiful you are,' he said softly, distinctly. 'Like a princess, straight and fine and strong as steel, an aristocrat from your elegant little feet to the top of your lovely head. All that a man could desire.'

Mesmerised, she waited. For a long, charged moment he stared at the pure contours of her face, his own gaze searching, almost wary, noting the shifting play of colour and textures in the huge, blue-green eyes trapped by his. Petra made no protest as he kissed her, his mouth gentle, and then suddenly hard.

A primal, inborn need held her still as he stepped out of his clothes and came down beside her. Without a will of her own, acquiescent, almost submissive, she let him touch her with his knowing hands, his experienced mouth, waiting quietly for the dark force, the upwelling of primitive desire. When it came she greeted it as an old enemy, yet surrendered to it, losing herself in the heated flood, the seduction of his voice and his hands and his mouth, the blatant response of her body.

He knew so well what to do, how to play on the responses she could not withhold; she had forgotten, she thought dazedly as he rediscovered the pleasure-points he had brought into being, just how fatally skilled he was at this, how his mouth on her breasts, demanding yet tender, could send her into some other dimension, turn her from a stone princess into a creature who lived only through her senses, experiencing for these maddened minutes nothing that was not caused by him.

When at last he moved over her she gasped, 'Yes, Caine, oh, please,' aware of the leaping lights of triumph in his eyes, yet unable to resist.

It was just as it had always been, the incandescent pleasure of being taken over and possessed by Caine's dark masculinity, her agonised movements as she strove for the unattainable, and then the explosion of sensation, pure yet carnal, as he took from her the control of her own body and personality. Then came the release, the slow drifting down, dreamy and sated with pleasure, until the first pangs of shame, sharp and piercing as a spear, began to penetrate the golden haze.

'Now,' Caine said, making no attempt to mute the triumph in his tone. 'Now, princess, admit that there is nothing to be ashamed of in that. You were not the only one lost to everything but desire.'

CHAPTER TEN

PETRA opened her eyes to a face alight with unrepressed satisfaction, and the hateful tears came like the rain outside, hard and fast.

Through them she heard Caine swear, a vicious monosyllable, then he moved over and pulled her into his arms, cradling her against the strength of his body, his cheek on the top of her head, slowly rubbing her long, naked back as she wept. Shudders racked her body; immediately a long arm swept up the sheet and the blankets, enclosing them both in a cocoon of warmth. Hating herself, hating him, she tried to pull away from the potent heat of his embrace.

He put a stop to that by tightening his arms. 'Hush,' he said evenly. 'Stop it, Petra, you'll make yourself sick. Go to sleep now, princess, go to sleep...'

When she woke it was still daytime, and outside the rain was falling steadily with the same dull persistence. Caine was sleeping on his side facing her, as though he felt he had to watch her all the time, even in sleep.

It's starting all over again, she thought in blind terror.

She had sold her soul to the devil, surrendered all control to him. Just like her mother, she was unable to fight the hungry needs of her body. Oh, she loved Caine, loved him with every ounce of her being, but, even in the ecstasy that had racked him the night before, he had said nothing about love.

And always poisoning her mind was the knowledge that if he loved her he would have believed her when she'd told him that Uncle Laurence had lied. He did not believe her, so he could not love her. This desire was all that she would get from him, but, sweet and satisfying as it was, it was not enough. Perhaps she was greedy.

After all, she was married to him, she had his promise to be faithful...

It tasted like ashes in her mouth.

A bitter, aching humiliation ate into her bones. From now on Caine would be able to look at her and know that whenever he wanted her he had only to crook his finger and she would come; she had no resistance at all to his brand of dark enchantment.

When she began to ease from the bed his hand shot out and grabbed her wrist. She stayed still; it was too late to resist. A few seconds later his eyes opened, slightly dazed, then immediately alert, sharpening as they focused on her in an intent, unsettling look.

'Trying to run away?' he drawled. 'I'll cure you of that even if I have to chain you to my wrist.'

Her smile was a masterpiece of irony. Looking at the angular contours of his beloved face, she decided with a determination which had its origin in naked self-preservation that he would never learn from her that it was the strongest bonds of all, those of love, which held her captive.

'No,' she said quietly. 'I won't run away again.'

He looked quizzically at her, his gaze sharpening as he scanned the contours of her face. 'What's the matter?'

'Nothing.'

He didn't accept her denial, that was clear, but he let it go for the moment. Yawning, he pulled her into the circle of his arms and kissed her—a stamp of possession, insisting that she respond before he let her go. 'How's your head?'

'Fine. No headache. I feel good.'

He touched the bump with a gentle finger. 'Yes, it's gone down a little, although it's turning some interesting colours. I think it's time we had something to eat.'

'I'll get it,' she offered.

'No.' He stretched magnificently, enjoying with open, arousing pleasure the play of his muscles, the virile male strength that she craved for. 'You look a bit transparent around the eyes. Stay there, and I'll get it.'

He was very considerate with her as they ate toast and bacon, although a little remote. Petra hated that withdrawal.

After they had washed the dishes he asked permission to use the telephone. She gave it, and ran upstairs, where she stripped the sheets and pillowcases from the bed, replacing them with clean ones. Yet it seemed to her that the scent of their passion still permeated the room, even the house.

If only she had somewhere to go! Anything would be better than sitting around remembering what it had been like to find her flawed paradise in his arms. Perhaps she could go to work. She walked across to the window, and stood staring out, her eyes dilated in her fragile face.

In the last few minutes the rain had eased. The cloud covering had lifted a little, and there was a hopeful brightness around the horizon. Petra ran down the stairs, hearing Caine's voice, cool and crisp and incisive as he conducted his conversation on the phone. Outside, the air was moist and cool, fragrant with the scents of growing things and the earthy dankness of the soil. Petra bent to pull a couple of stray weeds, and walked down the drive to the letter-box.

Only a circular and a letter from an old friend. Sighing, she walked back to the house which was her prison and her castle.

Caine was still remote for the rest of the day, but kind, insisting that she rest, and in the afternoon taking her to her own doctor for another check-up to make sure that she was recovering well.

That night they made love once more—a wild, fierce mating that made savages of them both, until, exhausted, Petra slept in his arms again, waking to a morning when the sun shone benignly over the sodden garden, and blackbirds and little olive-green white-eyes flirted in the camellia bushes while fantails flitted from branch to branch.

She woke alone. There was no sign of Caine, no indication of where he had gone, so she showered the scent and the feel of him from her skin, cleaned the taste of him from her mouth, and made herself a sandwich and coffee, taking them out into the sun where she stood with her face lifted to its rays, her eyes closed.

She almost didn't hear the telephone, but its summons broke through the dazed acceptance of her mood, and with a sigh she went back into the house.

It was Caine. 'I have to finish off something,' he said abruptly. 'I'll be away until the end of the week.' A moment's pause before he said on a harsh, indrawn breath, as though the words were torn from him, 'Miss me just a little, princess.'

Petra spent the following three days in a kind of unholy limbo. Caine didn't come—she didn't know whether he was still in New Zealand, or whether he had flown back to America. It was only with the greatest effort of willpower that she managed to function at all.

But gradually, as she worked in the garden, she began to realise that he had done something for her. His forthright insistence that he wanted her as much as she wanted him, and his open, fierce desire, expressed in the pagan forcefulness of their lovemaking, somehow convinced her in the innermost parts of her soul that he did not put her in the same category as her mother. As the lonely days dragged by she felt clean for the first time in years. Gone was the shame and the pain, the conviction that she was a slave to a rampant sexuality.

What she felt for Caine was much greater than that, although the soaring desire was part of it. She loved him. It was as simple and as complex as that. Passion was only part of it, and by no means the least part, but it was indivisibly mingled with tenderness and affection, respect and fascination, in the deep mystery that the world called love. Her mother had sought this in the

arms of her many lovers, but Petra had found it. And
seeing this, knowing that her love would never die, she
could see that her mother had led a tragic life, always
seeking, always disappointed.

When he comes back, she vowed, refusing to even
allow the possibility that he might not be intending to
come back—for how could she ask trust from him if she
couldn't give it?—when he comes back I won't cry because he doesn't love me. I'll take what he does feel,
and we'll build on that.

On Saturday morning she opened the newspaper, and
read to her incredulous surprise that Stanhope's was
going public, under the aegis of Caine Fleming, who
now controlled it due to the retirement of Laurence
Stanhope.

It is perhaps surprising that the man who took
Patience Computers to its present worldwide emi-
nence should be prepared to oversee the welfare of
Stanhope's, small beer as it must be for him, but there
is a family connection, and the firm will definitely gain
because of it.

Petra gave a choked little gasp and read on.

Laurence Stanhope is unavailable for comment and
Caine Fleming has refused to make a statement, but
it is believed that this does not affect his career path.
He is on a personal visit to New Zealand.

It went on to give a careful, potted history of the firm;
reading between the lines Petra thought that the journalist trod skilfully, intimating that it was time for some
sort of shake-up in the firm without stating flatly that
it was in trouble. A troubled frown creasing her brow,
her eyes lingered on the newspaper photograph of Caine
that accompanied it. Even through the poor repro-
duction his vitality, the arrogant strength, the unyielding
purpose of the man blazed forth.

Why had he done this? Caine was not a magnanimous man, she thought with an internal shiver. He had made it plain that it wouldn't worry him unduly to reduce her aunt and uncle to penury. Why had he let Uncle Laurence off so easily? And where was he? Surely he would be back with her soon?

But he didn't return.

A few days later David invited her out to dinner at a small new restaurant. Petra accepted, and during the dinner told him that she wouldn't be seeing him again.

'Fleming?' he asked perceptively.

'Yes.'

He nodded. 'I can't say I'm surprised. It's all right, I won't ask any questions, but I'd like to think that we're friends enough for you to know that I'll always be there if you need me.'

She smiled with great affection at him.

Back at home he turned into the driveway, and asked, 'Whose is the BMW?'

Petra's heart lurched. She peered out through the window, and sure enough it was Caine who was unfolding himself from the front seat, moving with a feral, deadly purpose across the drive.

'What the hell——?' David said, getting out himself with surprising speed.

But it was Caine's hand that jerked the door on Petra's side open, Caine's fingers that fastened with numbing strength around her arm and almost dragged her out.

'That hurts,' she said jerkily. 'Caine, please——'

His teeth flashed in the darkness. 'Sorry,' he snapped, clearly not. He looked across at David, and said in a flat, lethal voice, 'Get the hell out of here.'

Visibly confounded, David looked at Petra, who began, 'Caine——'

'Go home,' Caine interrupted, each word stark with threat. 'And don't bother coming back.'

Petra drew a painful breath.

Before she could speak David said angrily, 'I'll go if Petra tells me to go, and not before.'

Caine's voice dropped. 'Get lost.' His stance altered imperceptibly, but terrifyingly. Menace crackled like forked lightning about him. Hands cupped by his sides, he looked lethal and primitively efficient. To Petra, staring up at him in the moonlight, he was like some great hunting beast, longing for his prey to make some movement so that he could tear it apart.

Quickly she said, 'David, go home, please. This has nothing to do with you.'

'Only,' David responded grimly, 'in that any man has the duty to make sure that any woman is not hurt.'

Caine said in the silky voice of ultimate fury, 'It isn't Petra I feel like hurting, you fool, it's you. I find I have very little patience left when it comes to her lover, and just so that you know I mean it let me tell you that she and I are married again, so she has no further need of you.'

Petra closed her eyes.

Startled, David looked from the silver and ebony carved mask that was Caine's face to Petra's, still and cold and withdrawn beneath the thin light of a new moon. 'Petra?'

'Yes,' she confirmed, the word hurting her throat.

David looked keenly at her, but nodded. 'Very well, I'll go,' he said. 'But just to get one thing clear, Fleming, Petra and I are friends; we have never been lovers.'

With cold, controlled menace, Caine said, 'It doesn't matter. What matters is that she is not now available to you.'

He stood arrogantly waiting, until with a last troubled look David got back into his car and set it in motion.

'You can let me go,' Petra informed Caine thinly, 'I'm not going to run away.'

'You've done nothing but run away in one form or another,' he snapped, taking the keys from her nerveless hand, 'ever since we got married. But this is it, I've had enough. I'm not going to let you do it any more.'

Inside the sterile and unconvincing sanctuary of her home he closed the door and shot the bolt home. Dressed in casual trousers and a clear gold shirt, the sleeves rolled up to show his forearms, still vibrating with barely repressed anger, he was big and dark and dominating, too big for her room, too big for her life.

Petra stood for endless seconds, her lashes hiding the blue-green depths of her eyes. When he turned she said bluntly, 'I have not slept with David.'

'You spent the night before I asked you to marry me with him,' he stated, not attempting to hide the contempt colouring his tone.

Her jaw dropped. 'How did you know?'

'Because,' he told her, showing his teeth, 'I came here afterwards. The place was obviously empty, so I followed a hunch. I arrived outside his flat just in time to see you walk through the door with him.'

She remembered the car lights hurtling down the street as she had gone in through the door, the screech of brakes and the sudden acceleration.

'Yes,' he said remotely. 'I went home and drank myself into a stupor.'

She bit her lip. 'David came in for a cup of coffee, and while he was here someone rang and refused to speak to me. Just listened, and breathed. It wasn't the first time it had happened. I was frightened, especially when the phone rang again. So David insisted I go home with him.' She shivered, more at the look of sheer fury in his face than at remembered fear. 'I'm glad I did, as the answerphone was activated five more times during the night.'

'Have you contacted Telecom?'

'Yes, but he hasn't rung since then.' She searched his face for some signs of softening, of belief. To no avail; he had reined in his anger, the threat that had intimidated David, but there was no sign of emotion in his harsh features. Striving to overcome hopelessness, she went on, 'But I didn't sleep with David. I never have.'

He was watching her with a cool, analytical gaze that made her shrivel, but instead of sneering he said thoughtfully, 'I see. I wondered. When we made love you certainly seemed—almost virginal. I wondered if that was part of your appeal, the rare ability to seem fresh and innocent with each man. Have there been any other men, princess?'

'You have no right to ask me that question. We were divorced.'

'Not by my choice,' he reminded her, his voice very hard. 'Why *did* you divorce me?'

She was pale. 'I thought you might want to marry again.'

'I thought it was because *you* wanted to.'

Unable to answer, she shook her head. He said roughly, 'I told myself I didn't care, that I didn't want a woman who saw only my bank balance when she looked at me.'

'Why did you come back?' she asked, holding her breath.

'I've told you.'

'No,' she said. 'You've told me lies, or excuses. I want the truth.'

The silence stretched between them, taut, humming with significance. Finally he said, 'I came back because I've never been able to get you out of my mind.'

'And you wanted to punish me for that,' she concluded flatly.

Another shrug. 'Possibly. Oh, hell, yes, I suppose so. When I first saw you under the moon on your eighteenth birthday I felt as though every forbidden dream I'd ever had had just come true. You were far too young—I didn't even have to kiss you to realise that. You were so bloody innocent. And even though I realised that your uncle had invited me for some ulterior reason—he hated all that I stood for—I wanted you, and so I took you.'

'I didn't seduce you,' she said starkly. 'Not so that we'd be married, anyway.'

His mouth twisted. 'I should never have said that. What happened was as much my fault as yours. I was ten years older than you, old enough to be able to control myself. But I wanted you so much ... So I let myself be persuaded into marrying you.'

'And we were happy,' she said, not looking at him.

'We lived in a fool's paradise,' he corrected harshly. 'All you felt was a powerful lust, but I hoped it would eventually turn into love. Until I discovered that you knew exactly why your uncle had asked me to your birthday party.' The soft snarl sent shudders running down her spine. 'Until I realised that all that innocent passion, that flaming desire, was a sham. I thought you'd sacrificed yourself for your uncle and aunt. God knows, I despised myself enough for falling head over heels in lust like a randy adolescent, but to discover that I'd been conned by a sweet face and a delectable little body and an overwhelming sense of obligation—it was too much. I felt like murdering you all.'

One stride took Petra across to him; grabbing him by the upper arms, her fingers digging into the resistant muscle, she shook as hard as her strength would allow, staring up into his face with furious eyes.

'You listen to me,' she stormed. 'And make sure you hear, and that you understand. I had no idea what Uncle Laurence wanted from you, none at all. *I did not know!* What the hell do you think I am, to believe that I'd have married a man I didn't love to keep my uncle solvent? I'm not such a fool!'

He surveyed her passionate face with chilling coolness. 'I know,' he said. 'I know that you had no idea what Stanhope was doing.'

Her hands fell away as she searched his face with painful intensity, trying to see what was beneath the dark, closed mask. 'Did you ask Uncle Laurence?' she asked slowly, for some reason hurt that he would believe her uncle when he had not believed her. 'When you organised this business with Stanhope's?'

'No. I think he would have continued to lie to me, don't you? You convinced me—when you told me that I'd left because I was disgusted by your passionate nature. If you believed that, then you obviously didn't know anything about your uncle's manoeuvrings. So he lied when he told me you did.'

Her eyes filled with shadows, hiding her thoughts. 'So you...had to have proof. You didn't lo—trust me enough to believe me.'

'After I'd lent him the money,' Caine explained in an even tone that told her nothing, 'when it was all signed and sealed, he told me that you knew exactly why he'd agreed to the marriage. He intimated that you had sacrificed yourself for his well-being.' His mouth curled. 'He spoke glowingly of your loyalty, and how useful that would be to an up-and-coming man like me. As well as making it crudely obvious that I needed your breeding and style to make me socially presentable.'

'And you believed him?' She looked at him in astonishment. 'You honestly believed that I would be such a total idiot?'

'It seemed likely,' he said tonelessly. 'There was certainly no doubt about your loyalty, or the affection and gratitude you felt for them. After all, you did it again, a few days ago. Married me because I threatened him.'

Petra hesitated. Now, she thought, aware that this was the greatest gamble she had ever taken. Now, you have to tell him *now*. 'I married you both times because I love you. I don't know why he lied to you—perhaps he disliked you so much that he wanted to strike at your arrogance in the only way he knew how. Perhaps it was some kind of...obscure claim, if you like, on me.'

'I see.' Caine spoke in his most aloof voice.

With a sincerity so stark that it was compelling, Petra went on, 'I fell in love with you that first night, while I was standing on the bridge watching you walk across the garden. Oh, it was a childish, immature love, but as much as I was able to I loved you. I have never been so incandescently happy as I was while we were married, never before, never since.'

His face was carved in teak, forbidding, completely unyielding. Petra knew that she had lost, that he didn't love her, refused to allow himself to. An ache of despair ravaged her heart.

And then she stiffened. Last time pride and humiliation had dictated her actions, but not now. She was sure that somewhere deep inside him there was the key which would permit him to acknowledge that the obsession he resented so blackly was love. She had to try to reach it.

Knowing that she must risk everything, fearing that without her final throw of the dice he would leave her, she said quietly, 'I have never stopped loving you. Why do you think there has been no one else?'

'I wondered.' He closed his eyes for a moment, as though she saw too much. When he opened them they were dark, as dark as the emotions she saw in them. 'It's the same for me. Oh, there have been other women—a few. But every time I kissed one it was your sweet, laughing mouth that I felt, you I wanted ... So I decided to come back and see if I could rid myself of this drug in my bloodstream. If you were married, well——' the broad shoulders moved in a shrug '—I'd see how it was going, possibly have an affair with you.'

She made a soft gasp, and the blunt self-derision intensified in his expression. 'It happens,' he said, watching her closely. 'But when I saw you—I couldn't believe that my lovely, laughing, passionate girl had iced over, been imprisoned by a glossy, brittle mask of sophistication. You looked at me without a glimmer of emotion, and I wanted to smash through that calm, serene mask, to force

the real Petra Fleming out of hiding. I tried to get at
you with insults, but you just looked at me with those
lovely blank eyes, impervious, refusing even to justify
your way of life.' He overbore her sound of protest,
ending ruthlessly, 'You were totally lacking in animation, a beautiful, gracious, exquisitely mannered
puppet. A stone princess.'

'So you married me.'

His mouth twisted. 'I thought you were sleeping with
Carey.'

Petra's brows shot up. Had it been jealousy—or possessiveness that had led to that decision? 'So?'

'I was so bloody jealous I would have done anything
to get you out of his bed. It sounds melodramatic, but
I wanted to kill him—and you, even though I knew I
had no right to object. But that was when I knew I had
to marry you again, and I used your fears for your uncle
to force you to do it.'

She said quietly, 'Caine, if I didn't love you, you could
have done your worst to Uncle Laurence and I still
wouldn't have married you. Morally, I owe you that
money. If it hadn't been for me you would never have
lent it to Uncle Laurence. I'll pay you back as much as
I can.'

'Don't be a fool,' he retorted angrily.

She lifted her brows, staring him down, and he swore,
and said thickly, 'Don't look at me like that, as though
I'm a peasant and you are a princess. You were so bloody
composed about the whole thing! It was clear that I
didn't affect you in the least. That first night up north
I couldn't sleep—I was desperate for you—but you lay
in bed beside me, and you were a million miles away.'

She smiled mirthlessly. 'I developed that armour because you had hurt me so much I had to find some way
of keeping my emotions hidden.'

'There was more to it than that, wasn't there? When
we made love you came to life in my arms with the ardour
I remembered, the passion that's haunted me through

all the years. Yet the next day you were locked away
again in your ice tower, the princess beyond reach, under
a spell. Why? Surely it wasn't that you still believe I
class you with your mother?'

She looked up, met his keen glance, and the colour
flooded her face.

When she said nothing he probed, 'Afterwards you
wept as though your heart would break. You wouldn't
tell me why, but that had something to do with it, didn't
it? What was it, Petra?'

'I didn't think you were ever going to be able to trust
me. I had tried to convince you that I hadn't betrayed
you, and you didn't believe me. If you loved me, even
a little, you would have at least tried to believe me,' she
said quietly.

'I didn't want to love you,' he declared restlessly, his
face suddenly bleak. 'I tried so hard not to.'

Petra scanned his beloved countenance with compassion and love. 'Because you were almost pro-
grammed to believe that everyone wants payment of
some sort or the other? That's why you found it so easy
to believe I'd been part of a plot to trap you, wasn't it?
First your parents and then the Andersons, demanding
payment for something that should have been given
freely, without thought of reward. I understand now why
you were so angry when you thought I had married you
for money, but at the time I couldn't believe you'd be
so blind. That's when I began to wonder whether you
thought I was like my mother, that my blatant appetites
disgusted you. I still think it was a reasonable as-
sumption. You changed after we had made love the first
time, became distant, and—almost taunting. And after
that first time you never lost control, although you used
to make sure I did.'

'You could never disgust me,' he said, the banked
flames in his eyes beginning to lick high. 'I changed because, I suppose, I wanted to punish you a little for

sending Stanhope along with his metaphorical shot-gun and his talk of it being my duty to marry you.'

'But I didn't,' she asserted urgently.

He smiled ironically. 'I believe you. I behaved like an arrogant swine. And yes, one reason I reacted so badly to his lies was because I was sick of being bought and sold, of paying for my chances. A month before I'd met you the Andersons had made their play for their reward, and I suppose I was essentially cynical.'

Petra's heart ached for the child he had been—bartered, never loved for himself alone. Like an eagle in a pack of barnyard fowls, no one had known what to make of him, not even the Andersons who had sensed his potential.

'What was the other reason?' she asked.

'I loved you.'

Petra's heart slammed into triple time, but the fear that it was over, that his love had died almost still-born, dried her mouth.

'So,' he said calmly, 'what do we do now?'

'I don't know,' she replied, hoping against hope that from the shadows of the past they could pluck some sort of security, some joy. Could his desire and her need be enough for their happiness, or would she always feel that she was being short-changed?

'Is it too late for us, Petra? Have I made too many mistakes?'

Trembling, she said softly, 'No, it's not too late.'

He smiled, the old wicked smile of possession and passion. 'Good,' he said.

'Caine,' she asked quietly, 'what do you feel for me?'

He closed his eyes, shutting her out, then opened them. Petra thought she was being burned by the crystalline fire that glittered in their depths, but, as she watched, the old, protective transparence was replaced by warmth, a steady, glowing heat that told her what he was going to say before the slow words came forth.

'Dear heart, my princess, I have never stopped loving you. Never. That's why I left you the first time; the pain was so great I couldn't stand to be in the same country as you. That's why I've never married again, even though I wanted a wife and children, because the wife had to be you, and the children had to be yours...'

Petra knew she should be happy, but was unable to experience it; the iron-bound restraint of the last years was still in place, blocking any open response. But deep inside her emotions were kindling, and she felt the first trickles of the thaw.

'I want to make love,' she stated, flushing but determined.

A muscle flicked in the lean angularity of his jaw, the tiny betrayal lending even more strength to the severe line of his mouth. 'Are you sure?' he asked deeply. 'I don't want to rush you into bed unless you're ready for it. Last time I tried to show you that there was nothing of disgust or of contempt in the way I feel for you.'

Colour flowed exquisitely through her skin. 'You did. While you were away I began to understand.'

'If you want to wait, I'm happy to. I love you—I can't say that the making love doesn't matter, because it does, it's the nearest I'll ever get to heaven; but even if you were unable to make love I'd still love you, still want you back.'

Adoring him for his consideration, she smiled mistily. 'I love you,' she said with soft invitation. 'And you've tried very hard to convince me that desire is a normal and necessary part of love.'

He hesitated, then swung her up into his strong arms and took her with him into the bedroom.

This time it was different. This time he undressed her slowly, with loving hands, telling her how beautiful she was, describing in graphic detail exactly what the sight of her slender, nude body did to him, until colour ran like wildfire through her skin.

'Like living satin,' he murmured, kissing the tender spot where her neck met her shoulder. 'Smooth and silky, warmed by life. I've never forgotten how lovely you are...'

Her insecurities prompted her breathed denial. 'I'm too thin.'

'Not for me, you're perfect for me, you're all that I've ever wanted.'

Petra gasped as his teeth marked her flesh lightly, a shiver of sensation arrowing through her from the base of her throat. Delicately he touched his tongue to the faint redness, banishing the tiny hurt, and slid his hands up under her breasts, plumping them out, his eyes devouring their soft curves until the colour that had been fading flared up once more.

'I like the way you blush all over. Undress me,' he murmured against her mouth.

Hands shaking with a combination of eagerness and delight, she undid the buttons of his shirt. She wanted this more than anything, and for reasons other than the desire that was beating like a flashfire through her. It was like the first time all over again, fresh and untarnished, yet enriched by their love and their new-found trust in each other.

This time, she thought exultantly as her hand slid across the broad expanse of his chest, lingering on the flexing muscles, sliding through the springy hair, this time she could indulge her passion and her love to the full, and not be left with the acrid taste of shame and disillusion afterwards.

She had always loved touching him, stroking his sleek hide with caressing fingers; it was one of the things she had found totally unacceptable about herself, that she could forget the tenets of her aunt's teaching and be so bold, glorying in the differences between Caine's lithe masculine body and her own softer one.

Now she forgot everything in the pleasure of pressing hot, open-mouthed kisses across his chest until she found the little nipples and teased them with her tongue. They hardened, and he laughed deep in his chest, and put her on the bed, coming down beside her like an avenging angel, his face already drawn into the dark lineaments of passion.

'Finish what you started,' he demanded, running a lean hand from her throat to her breast, stopping so close to the nipple that she felt it peak, the delicious little sensation searing through her to collect with other sensations in the fork of her body.

She slid her hand down the taut midriff to the front of his trousers and stripped him, her hands lingering, her eyes half closed with desire, the lids drooping heavily. He was magnificent, aroused male, as untrammelled and as primitive as a fertility god, his gleaming body sleek and taut against the sheets.

'You are beautiful,' she murmured, adoring him, her voice shaking as she touched him with trembling fingertips.

'Nowhere near as beautiful as you.' The hand that cupped her breast moved, and his head swooped, dark against the soft pinkness of her skin, and his mouth found the aching tip of her breast. No longer did she try to control the sensations that rioted through her, no longer did she have to search his face for the first faint glimmerings of disgust.

Arching joyously to the demands of his hands and his mouth, her own as ravenous, as inciting, she followed him into a country she had never known, where love was the ruler and nothing else existed. The primal hunger Petra had so feared grew, encompassing them both, until finally they were hurled together over the unimaginable edge into a new world, freed from the shackles of the past, forging new bonds in the promise of the future.

In the dreamy aftermath she was aware of their mingled heartbeats, the slow slide of sweat-slicked skin over sweat-slicked skin, the tiny sensual ache deep inside, a faint melancholy because it had been so wonderful and now it was over.

Caine lifted himself on to his elbows, but she made a soft murmur of protest, and her arms tightened across his back.

'I'm too heavy,' he said, and moved over, scooping her against him so that they lay locked together.

After another dreamy period he whispered, 'Ghosts laid, my dearest lady, my princess?'

'Oh, yes,' she replied sleepily, tilting her head to look into his face, her own soft and radiant with the pleasure of loving him. 'Are yours?'

He looked younger, the severe lines of his features softened, although the underpinnings of bone, the high sweep of his cheekbones and the strength of his jaw would always be austere. But the same miracle that had worked for her had touched him, too, and there was a happiness too deep and too obvious to be constrained in his expression. The crystalline eyes would never be soft, but the flames that had irradiated them left their warmth behind, and she saw the love openly revealed in them, as well as in his lazy smile.

'Well and truly vanquished. Gone with the wind. Are you going to be happy living in America with me?'

'I'd be happy living on the moon with you,' she vowed.

He laughed softly. 'You'll like San Francisco, it's one of the most civilised cities in the world. But we'll spend a lot of our time in New Zealand. With the telecommunication link-ups we have now I can stay in touch. And I'm thinking of easing back on my workload. Patience needs a different approach now; it needs to consolidate the work I've done. And I prefer starting things, working on new aspects of technology, to the more boring corporate duties.'

'You have something in mind?'

'Oh, there are all sorts of angles,' he said vaguely, his eyes frankly devouring as they swept her face. 'We'll talk about them when I come back down to earth. Did you know that when you are naked your eyes are the softest, clearest blue-green, like the very best aquamarines? Would you like to keep the bach, or have I made it ugly for you?'

'Nothing,' she said passionately, 'could make it ugly for me. I love it, because I found you again there. And it would be a good place for children.'

'Were you planning them soon?'

Petra grinned, frank mischief making her eyes dance. 'Neither of us is getting any younger, Caine. And, as I haven't been on the Pill since you left, and you haven't used any protection, I wouldn't be the least surprised if the first one is on its way already.'

'You wouldn't mind?'

She turned her head into his shoulder, kissing the long line of muscle, feeling it bulge as he moved, feeling other signs of stirring in the lean body. 'No,' she replied demurely. 'Not in the least. How about you?'

He kissed her again, yawned, stretched, and said huskily, 'I can think of nothing I'd like more.'

'Good.' She snuggled close in. Only one more thing remained to be cleared up. 'What made you decide to take over Stanhope's?'

His arms tightened. 'After we'd made love I lay awake for hours, accepting that eight years ago I'd been a cruel, bitter, unforgiving swine when I refused to believe you were innocent. I had never given you a chance, and it was because of me, because I'd so disillusioned you with my complete lack of trust, that you'd turned yourself into a stone princess. All these years I'd blamed you, but I was the one who failed you. I wanted to come to you with clean hands. So I left you—and God, it was hard—and flew up to Fiji to deal with Stanhope.'

She nodded. 'I knew you'd come back.'

'I should have told you what I was doing, but I was so sick of all the machinations in the background, of the dead hand of your uncle... I'm sorry if I was thoughtless.'

Petra gave a ghost of a laugh, running her hand over the hard layer of muscle across his ribs. 'We probably needed the time apart. Don't ever do it again, though.'

'I swear.' His voice was deep and harsh with emotion. 'From now on, my dearest love, we're going to be closer to each other than the pages in a book.'

'I haven't thanked you for saving Uncle Laurence's bacon, either.'

'You don't have to. You love your aunt and uncle, and so they are important to me, too. Some time in the night after we made love I found myself wondering whether perhaps I disliked them so because you loved them. It was an unpleasant supposition, and one that made me take stock of myself and my emotions. Stanhope's should be able to pull itself out of the mire and see out another generation. Your uncle has retired with a golden handshake, so his future is assured.'

'And what,' she asked, her voice betraying by a tiny tremor that the subject was still a sore one, 'what about the money he owes you?'

'Oh, to hell with it!' But he was laughing, the brackets on either side of his mouth deepening as he told her, 'It's all organised. I've taken out that amount of shares in the wretched company, and I expect them to make me lots of money, and that is the last time I ever want to hear about that bloody loan! If it hadn't been for that we could have spent these last eight years happily making love and children and a good life together.'

'I doubt if we would have.' She traced the line of hair along his chest, her hand slender and graceful against the flexing muscles. 'Oh, we might have made something of our marriage, but I was too young, and even then I knew that we shouldn't have married. I'm glad we had these years apart. I matured in lots of ways. And we know each other better now, just as we know ourselves. I think we met each other too soon.'

'Perhaps you're right.' He kissed the tip of her ear, his breath an erotic little summons. 'Now go to sleep.'

As she lay against him in the kindly dark, listening to the soft rise and fall of his breath, Petra smiled, an enormous satisfaction irradiating her sleepy face. They had found each other at last. The future spread before them, rich with the promise of hope and love and laughter.

Her last thought as she drifted off to sleep was that the armour the stone princess once wore had been shattered by the forces of love and trust.

WORDFIND #8

```
A  U  C  K  L  A  N  D  T  Y  H  J  I  P
W  E  N  G  R  T  Y  I  O  W  D  F  K  R
G  N  S  K  U  O  Y  E  S  D  G  H  J  I
A  S  B  W  E  G  B  T  T  Y  I  D  N  N
N  A  D  R  E  E  D  Y  O  F  R  L  B  C
S  A  S  A  R  E  N  R  N  B  E  A  D  E
A  Q  W  E  E  T  W  R  E  B  C  N  C  S
Q  A  C  T  W  T  Z  A  T  Y  O  D  S  S
A  F  L  R  M  I  B  Y  L  A  N  U  A  T
F  A  E  T  A  Y  N  D  C  I  C  R  W  G
A  R  O  M  H  N  U  O  F  E  I  U  Q  K
R  A  S  H  J  K  C  A  P  R  L  P  X  J
A        F           E  Z  X  C  V  B  N  C  M
```

AUCKLAND   PETRA
CAINE   PRINCESS
CONVENIENCE   RECONCILE
DONALD   ROBYN
FLEMING   ROMANCE
NEW ZEALAND   STONE

Look for A YEAR DOWN UNDER Wordfind #9
in September's Harlequin Presents #1586
AND THEN CAME MORNING by Daphne Clair   WF8

**Relive the romance...
Harlequin and Silhouette
are proud to present**

by Request

A program of collections of three complete novels by the most
requested authors with the most requested themes. Be sure to
look for one volume each month with three complete novels by
top name authors.

In June: **NINE MONTHS** Penny Jordan
Stella Cameron
Janice Kaiser

**Three women pregnant and alone. But a lot can
happen in nine months!**

In July: **DADDY'S
HOME** Kristin James
Naomi Horton
Mary Lynn Baxter

**Daddy's Home... and his presence is long
overdue!**

In August: **FORGOTTEN
PAST** Barbara Kaye
Pamela Browning
Nancy Martin

**Do you dare to create a future if you've forgotten
the past?**

Available at your favorite retail outlet.

HARLEQUIN PRESENTS®

A Year DOWN UNDER

In 1993, Harlequin Presents celebrates the land down under. In September, let us take you to Sydney, Australia, in AND THEN CAME MORNING by Daphne Clair, Harlequin Presents #1586.

Amber Wynyard's career is fulfilling—she doesn't need a man to share her life. Joel Matheson agrees . . . Amber doesn't need just *any* man—she needs him. But can the disturbingly unconventional Australian break down her barriers? Will Amber let Joel in on the secret she's so long concealed?

Share the adventure—and the romance—of A Year Down Under!

Available wherever Harlequin books are sold.

SOLUTIONS TO
WORDFIND #8

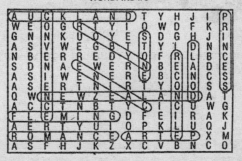